# To Taste

R. C. HUTCHINGS

Copyright © 2023 R. C. Hutchings

All rights reserved.

ISBN: 9798390727454

*To Shannon*

*I told you I would do it*

# CONTENTS

| | |
|---|---|
| *Acknowledgments* | i-ii |
| *Starters* | |
| The Tale of the Little Bakery | 1 |
| Address to a Table | 11 |
| Heinz Baked Beans | 26 |
| *Mains* | |
| When I Grow Up | 33 |
| Birth(day) | 60 |
| Podrido | 77 |
| *Desserts* | |
| Hard to Swallow | 95 |
| Being Hit by a Samosa on the Back of the Head | 119 |
| A Bowlful of my Love | 129 |
| *About the Author* | 144 |

# ACKNOWLEDGMENTS

I have to say, I'm starting to think this whole self-publishing malarkey was actually a good idea. Going down the expected route would have meant writing a ton of acknowledgments to all the people in the publishing world who helped me, and that is a rather overwhelming thought (one day, maybe – *hopefully* – this will be my reality and I'll be tearing up at my laptop. We'll cross that bridge when we come to it, eh?)

For now, let me just say that I'm incredibly grateful for all my friends and family who believed in me. You guys all know how much I've wanted to share my stories and make my dream of becoming a writer a reality. And guess what? It's *you* lucky folk who get to read said stories.

I also want to thank Paul Vlitos, my dissertation supervisor and creative writing lecturer from the University of Surrey. Back in 2017, I discovered an interest in food theory, which then inspired my dissertation, which then inspired *this* short story collection. Thank you for your advice, wisdom and your own literary criticism on the subject matter (those references really were invaluable.)

Finally, I want to thank myself for having the willpower and confidence to do something like this. Without me – funnily enough – this would not be possible.

You go, girl.

# THE TALE OF THE LITTLE BAKERY

Did you ever hear about the little bakery in Hassau? It was once owned by Mrs Kolb, an old, affable woman with hair like spider silk and a big, chocolate mole on the left side of her withered mouth. Yes, she was old, much too old to be running the *Bäckerei*, but people came from far and wide to sample her delectable delicacies. Fat loaves of *brot* fought for the limelight as eager customers entered through the beaten door with a *ting-a-ling*, mesmerised by warming, redolent aromas. Mrs Kolb and her two daughters would float about, clutching trays of buttery *puddingbrezel* or pillowy *bierocks*, smiling through the incessant back pain that comes with pursuing a culinary career. I should know – I've been through it myself. It's always worth it in the end, though. But back to Mrs

Kolb and her wizened fingers. Quite the magician she was – everyone said so. Stories flew about her apple cake, her paradisal *pumpernickel*, the bite of sour *kirsch* in her chocolate and cherry cake, slathered with sweet cream so airy people were convinced they got a little closer to heaven each time they took a bite. But the reason behind Mrs Kolb's unparalleled mastery? Brace yourself, for I shall tell you.

Mrs Kolb was a sweet woman – even the death of her equally saccharine husband failed to embitter her – and good intentions were the foundations of everything she did, the bread and butter – if you'll excuse the pun – of her enterprise. Consequently, our winsome little bakery was bestrewn with tiny shards of a certain kind of magic, magic made possible only by the unwavering commitment of loyal customers. Picture this: a mother and child walk into the bakery and are rendered speechless, enthralled by the displays, the heady scent of rising bread, the bijou cakes all glazed and glorious. The child wants everything and wants it now, anticipating the sublime sugar rush, and the mother is prepared to contend with said sugar rush if it means sampling even a morsel of the pastries at hand. Such was the effect of Mrs Kolb's creations, you see. The mother strikes up conversation with the proprietor, and there is a playful back-and-forth before Mrs Kolb delivers the unexpected ultimatum. Although, really, it is not so unexpected, and perhaps not an ultimatum, rather a natural conversational pivot.

"It's been an absolute pleasure, Frau Strossmayer, but before you go, won't you give us a little cheer? Something to smile about? I'm sure you have some good news, you must do!" And even if Frau Strossmayer has been battling with relentless depression, or has recently caught her husband seducing the butcher's daughter down the road, or just yesterday had her house burgled, or is in the process of packing her excitable son off to boarding school because he is utterly ungovernable, Mrs Kolb's eager smile will be enough for her to dig deep and pluck something cheery from the dark recesses of her mind. These anecdotes, these joyous accounts of good fortune and favour were the dashes of baking soda in Mrs Kolb's creations. Without the powerful words of the punters, their zeal and enthusiasm and willingness to disclose the happiest of happenings, the goods would not pack so much punch. It was the secret ingredient; Mrs Kolb and her daughters thrived on confessions of contentment, and in turn the pastries and the breads and the cakes and the pies would ooze with the same delight.

"How delicious!" Frau Strossmayer exclaims

as she exits the bakery with her boy and her bun, which is already dismantled, dustings of icing sugar wafting as she walks.

The bakery, thus, became the heartbeat of Hassau, enveloped by a celestial glow of goodness. On the one hand it's an endearing image; on the other, a tad nauseating. Speaking of sickness, one fateful day arrived during which Irma, the eldest and more experienced of Mrs Kolb's daughters, fell ill. Fortunately for her, some unoccupied townswomen took turns to tend to the sick baker. Unfortunately for Mrs Kolb and the business, a woman short meant they'd soon be short of earnings – they needed a new employee, and fast.

Enter Lorelei.

Lorelei was young, quick-witted, deft with her hands and a rolling-pin, old for her age. In short, a perfect match for the bakery. It all happened quite haphazardly; Mrs Kolb and her youngest daughter had been on the verge of closing up shop early, willing to exchange precious sales time for further preparations, but then Lorelei had rapped on the door with her pretty, forceful hand. The youngest daughter, wiping her hands on her apron, had opened the door. *Ting-a-ling*. Assistance had arrived.

"You are meticulous," Mrs Kolb remarked, watching as Lorelei pumped frost-white icing onto cookies, effortlessly wound snakes of dough into perfect plaits. Mrs Kolb was in no position to be picky, but the girl's dexterity filled her with relief. A trusting old woman, she revealed the secret ingredient to Lorelei and Lorelei smiled, enlivened, eager to get to work.

All was well – at least, for a time. Lorelei slotted neatly into the bakery like a blade in a knife block, oozing charm and charisma, buttering up even the most belligerent of buyers. She also had something neither Mrs Kolb nor Nina, the youngest daughter, had – a striking face. It was the cherry on top of the cake, you could say. An enchanting exterior, display after display of succulent sweet treats and an attractive face to welcome customers – there was no space for disappointment at the bakery, and the money began pouring in. Poor, helpless Irma lay at home, grey with fever, whilst sales at the bakery soared.

But then, gradually, things began to change.

It began when Irma returned to work. The illness had weakened her, but she was determined to be on her feet once again, couldn't stand the thought of lying helplessly in bed for another month. Lorelei remained front of house and became the new face of the bakery; sweet treats became synonymous with her comely features. The delicacies, however, soon began to take a turn for the worse. Old Mr Ehrhardt was the first to complain about the blandness of the butter biscuits, said he'd bought half a dozen and each was as tasteless as the last. Tasteless treats quickly became the tragic norm, and no matter how often the Kolbs reviewed their methods, scrutinising the efforts of one another with tense remarks, the baked goods remained underwhelming at best.

Soon the flavours began to mutate. The pastries, erstwhile claggy, inert, were imbued with a sudden, harsh prevalence of salt. The once sticky *kuchen* grew bone-dry, crumbs like tiny pebbles that grated against the soft flesh of expectant lips. Bitterness, like a thief in the night, crept in and dismantled the formula that had brought the bakery such sweet success, and though Lorelei appeared to grimace through it all, really, she was concealing a smile.

For she had wielded her own dark magic, ripping through the establishment like the gleeful tearing of soft bread before it drowns in the soup. Lorelei had traded hot buns for blistering secrets, confessions from the villagers that tainted the very air around them. Tales of jealousy, lies and deceit seeped into raw batter, curdling, fermenting, rendering the dough expendable. How she did this was a mystery. It was likely something to do with that alluring face, a face to whom one simply couldn't say no.

"You won't tell anyone, will you?" the local farmers would stammer, after confessing to lashing the crops of their competitors with sea salt and vinegar. Lorelei would put a finger to her rosebud mouth and shake her head, refusing the loose change the farmers held out in grubby, rough hands.

"Doesn't it feel better to have let it out?" Lorelei would simper to young girls, their faces pink from admitting to stealing from sweetshops, fantasising about married men during mass, spreading rumours about other youngsters they took a dislike to. She insisted the money was unnecessary, told them that the groceries were on the house if they had the courage to disclose feats of dark, adrenaline-induced spontaneity. As a result, not only did the customers suffer, but the bakery's income began to dwindle.

The stress was getting to old, Mrs Kolb. Irma, too, had been pulled back into isolation by her unrelenting illness, which started when she began to faint at work, putting off passers-by who had been willing to give the bakery a second chance despite its disparaging reviews. Soon Mrs Kolb was in bed beside Irma, and after that she was dead, and soon after that Irma accepted defeat and let death take her just as quietly, leaving only Nina – heartbroken, traumatised Nina – to stumble through the seemingly infinite working weeks with Lorelei. But there came a point when the money stopped, when the sound of a *ting-a-ling* would cause Nina to jump in surprise, when the myriad of stale, rotting food, like a chorus of ghosts, began to wail from the displays. Nina didn't want to go home to empty rooms and the cold air of failure, but she couldn't bear to spend any more time in the crumbling bakery either. She sat alone in the darkness and cried.

*Ting-a-ling.*

Nina looked up, heart hammering. Lorelei, with a wicked smile plastered on her pretty face, loomed over Nina, letting out a roar of laughter, and then began a rampage across the shop floor, swinging her arms, knocking the displays. Cakes catapulted. Buns bounced. Tortes, with their festering mould fell, cream splattering across the grimy floor. A cockroach shot out from the shadows and scampered the length of the shop. Nina, who couldn't remember the last time she had eaten, so nauseated from witnessing the decay and destruction around her, screamed. Lorelei bent down, the skeleton of something once edible sitting in her palm, and lifted it up to Nina's trembling mouth.

"Eat up, *schatzi*," she purred.

Nina, face spilling with tears, had no choice. But it was too much. The bakery was so full of dark deeds, so contaminated with death and horror that Nina began to choke, unable to stomach it. Writhing, her eyes rolled back and then she collapsed, crumbs lingering at her parted lips, finally still. Lorelei, with a triumphant smile, stood up and looked around, hands on her hips.

At last, she was able to close the *Bäckerei.*

And open her own business not long after.

People did not speak of Mrs Kolb and her two daughters. A quiet fear ran through the town, fear of unearthing what nobody wanted to unearth, and so the citizens of Hassau watched in apprehension as Lorelei unveiled her brand-new establishment, where the cakes, it transpired, were just as good, if not better, than those of old Mrs Kolb. The temptress deterred some, it must be said, but for those who were more optimistic, Lorelei welcomed them with open arms, and there was no funny business. *Strange, but thank goodness,* these punters would muse. *Perhaps it was old Mrs Kolb who had lost her touch and sent things spiraling out of control. She really had been past her prime.*

All's well that ends well. Lorelei's new venture thrived and remains to this day the hub of Hassau.
In my own unbiased upon, it's probably the best bakery around.

# ADDRESS TO A TABLE

It takes considerable strength not to throw up. The first sip, surprisingly, wasn't so bad. The whisky is ice-cool, warming slowly as it travels south. If I could just get over wanting to vomit, perhaps I could become an alcoholic. I can see why people get addicted. Once you're past the point of disgust, you come to appreciate how much it can numb the pain, I'm sure. We made a toast to the great bard, and now Alison, Ndella, Crew, Darsh and two guests I've never met before are ready for the night ahead. The momentary silence of the initial sips has been broken, and now Alice is already making a beeline for the kitchen.

"So, how did you guys meet?" Ndella asks Darsh.

"Wine and cheese night, actually," Darsh says. "She just couldn't take her eyes off me." Darsh laughs, glancing at me. His girlfriend is either too shy or not witty enough to make a comeback. She laughs, too, with her eyebrows raised to the roof.

"She'd had a bit too much wine then?" Ndella chips in, compensating for the lack of retaliation. In this moment I have a sudden loathing for Darsh, with his crisp, white shirt and his boat shoes and brazen attitude to most things. I turn the other way and there is Alice's friend, although I think she's also Ndella's friend as Alice told me they both met Jennifer at yoga. Or something like that.

"This flat is so lovely," Jennifer says. She looks like a young Julia Roberts, and I can instantly tell she is a Good Person.

"They don't come cheap, these Edinburgh flats," I say, instantly regretting it. She, too, has an English accent, but like most people at this gathering she's probably lived here for a considerable amount of time. Graciously, she takes what I've said as a statement of universal truth and hums loudly in agreement.

"Do you live locally?" she asks me, and suddenly a cool sweat forms on the back of my neck at the thought of an impending conversation. I take a long sip of Drambuie.

"I'm in Leith."

"*Nice*," she says, nodding enthusiastically. She does indeed know the city.

I don't know how Alice keeps everything so bloody *clean*, I really don't. She's been slaving away in here for the past God knows however many hours, but there isn't a crumb in sight. It's a testament to her as a person, I guess, it really is. Tidy up as you go along. *Do you think everyone will get on? I hope everyone will get on*. She's thinking aloud, wielding the masher. She's got mad wrist action – I should know. She sees me smirking to myself and looks sheepish. I kiss her on the top of her head. I tell her it's fine, Darsh's girlfriend is dispensable – we all know that – and Jenny would get on with anyone, and does she want another wee dram? I've perfected her accent by now. Just as I expected, she smiles in a sort of pained way, and then she's saying *go on*, but not to get her too drunk as she's the host. Pft. By midnight we'll be halfway through a ceilidh and no-one will care. Al just wants people to have a good time, bless her, even though just being in her presence is enough to make anyone happy – I should know. Suddenly, she says she's worried about Crew. I make myself useful. We say nothing for a minute or two, arranging dishes and serving spoons. *He doesn't look good, does he?* I agree with her. I ask her if she noticed that he went to the bathroom as soon as he got here. I bet if I go back out there, he'll be sitting by himself, not talking to anyone. Plus, he's got a face like a slapped arse. Al's eyes are glazed. She sighs. She wonders if maybe we shouldn't have invited him. Her shoulders sag with the weight of the neeps. Then she says we all need each other, and he was already bad before. *It sounds weird, too, but, like…we can sort of keep an eye on him here. He'd probably end up in a ditch somewhere at four am otherwise.*

Cindy tells them it was a theatre school in Surrey, and that it was as hectic as it sounds, though I'm pretty sure no-one is thinking that. I don't know why she said it. It makes her sound, well, as if everyone's been to theatre school, or that everyone cares. I mean, I do, obviously, but this is a table of thirty-somethings with proper jobs and she's working part-time backstage. I don't know why she isn't an actress – she's gorgeous enough, and she sure has enough to say.

"Wine's nice," I chip in.

Then Crew pipes up. He says, "Not sure why the fuck you guys are drinking wine when we should be drinking rusty nails." As if anyone asked for his opinion, the dipsomaniacal twat.

I let it slide. Alice and Ndella put in a lot of effort to make this a nice night. Plus, Doug's fucking fragile at the moment. I'm surprised he's here, but I'm glad to see him, even if he is staring into his glass.

Ndella asks if Crew wants to make them, and in true Ndella style, I can't tell if she's being sarcastic or not. Crew just lets out a weird laugh and takes another sip of his drink.

Cindy says she went to GSA, though I don't think she's the one to be breaking the awkward silence if I'm honest. Furthermore, what she said is just going to confuse the entire group because the only GSA these guys are familiar with is the Glasgow School of Art. I graciously untangle this information. A minute later, however, it becomes apparent that Cindy only graduated a year ago, and that's when Crew, again, decides to throw in his two cents. He really does choose his moments.

"Oh god, if you're fresh out of uni, how old are you?"

Cindy wavers, and I can see the hesitation on her face. She lowers her head, smiling, making it worse for herself because now she looks like a blushing sixteen-year-old girl.

"Twenty-two," I say. "Not sure how that's relevant to anything, though."

Crew whoops and the whole table shakes.

Then he becomes serious.

"You've got a lot to look forward to, Candy."

"Cindy," I correct.

Alice's friend, who looks like Natalie Portman, asks Ndella if Alice will be piping in the haggis, and Ndella grins and tells us to expect amazing things at any moment. Even Crew looks mildly interested. He really needs to be told about himself, honestly. *I* wouldn't do it in front of a group of friends though. That's not my style – that's his. Cindy takes my hand and squeezes it under the table. Half of me just wants to be back home in bed with her, making her moan, watching her eyes roll back.

Instead of playing the bagpipes, Ndella is marching to the sound of the speaker while I walk two steps behind her, holding the haggis. We're both giggling like schoolgirls, and it's so nice to see everyone beaming at us as we approach the table. There is a round of applause as I set the haggis down; I'm absolutely boiling now, but Ndella kisses me on the cheek and *I think maybe this is actually going pretty well. Everyone seems to be enjoying it.*

Cindy's very sweet. Bit worried about that relationship, but she seems like a nice girl. It's nice to have everyone together. It's been a while.

"Right, a toast," Ndella trills. She lifts her glass and graciously lowers her head. She is the queen, and we are her subjects. In this moment, I couldn't love anybody more.

"Hold on, the toasts come *after* the meal," Crew says, and I'm relieved to discover that he is, in fact, joking around. At least, it seems that way. These days, I can't really tell – Crew's whole personality is, I'm sorry to say, just…bitterness.

"How dare you interrupt me!" Ndella says playfully, the only person who has the ability to diffuse Crew's attempts at rocking the boat. He snorts, looks down at his plate and lets his head loll to one side.

"As I was saying…" Ndella pauses dramatically. "Fair fa' your honest, sonsie face."

Everybody chuckles, though I'm not sure whether Cindy knows the reference (she seems very young, and I don't think there's a Scottish bone in her body. She looks a little bit south Asian – she's got this lovely dark hair and these gorgeous cat-like eyes. I must ask her what make-up she uses.)

"No, don't worry, I'll spare you all the address. I know we're here to celebrate Robbie, but I don't think I have the mental capacity to recite eight stanzas. Although we're not just here for him, are we? No." The last word comes quickly, before Crew has a chance to drop another sarcastic comment. "I'd like to toast to Alice, because she is the fucking best, the love of my life, and the provider of this food."

I hate the fact that my face turns red so quickly. We clink glasses. Ndella is beaming at me.

"A toast to old friends…" Ndella gestures towards Darsh, Crew and Doug. "…new friends…" Cindy and Jenny smile. "Wait, that's it, that's all I got. Anymore for anymore?"

"You killed it," Darsh says, nodding with approval.

"Thank you all for coming." It's only right of me to add something. "This is nice. Really nice."

*This is nice. Really nice.* You know what would be nice? A fucking hammer to my head – I'd rather that than pretend it's all sunshine and roses.

"Jen hasn't been in Edinburgh long," Alice is telling Darsh's child-bride.

"Four months or so," Jen says. She has the demeanor of somebody who isn't out to impress anybody, who doesn't actually care, who just came for the food and wine. She looks like Jennifer Garner and is dangerously gorgeous.

"What do you do?" Darsh asks, ready to gauge if he's the one in the room earning the most money.

"I'm a curator, actually," Jen replies.
Surprising use of the word 'actually'. She's both dangerously gorgeous and, perhaps, diffident. "I work at the Fruitmarket."

"Ah, yeah, the Fruitmarket," Darsh says, though he's never been to an art gallery in his life.

Jen nods enthusiastically, then moves a stray piece of hair from her face. "I'm really enjoying it. We're working on a lot of community projects at the moment. I've been loving the exhibitions *and* there's a real involvement with the university; it's never boring."

"And whereabouts are you living?" Candy asks.

Who the fuck cares? Who honestly gives a flying fuck, or a running fuck, or any other kind of fuck? Why not ask her about her favourite artists? If she moved to the city for the job or if she moved to the city and then *found* the job? And if it were the latter, why did she move to the city? Does she believe museums are a respite from commercialism or a breeding ground for the selfie-taking wannabe marketers, trading experiences for likes and paid partnerships? Is she single?

"Just off Marchmont Road."

Doug has almost finished his drink. He hasn't been present for the duration of this conversation, and I don't think he's been present for most of the evening. His face is flushed, drawn, lips dry, stubble gathering around them. And no-one gives a damn.

"Did you guys all meet at uni?" Candy asks. When she speaks it's like the room suffers a temporary power cut.

"Yeah, we did." Everybody looks at Doug. He's looking at his plate as if the words that just materialised were not his.

"That's so cute. And also really admirable because I guess it must be super hard to see friends when you're in your thirties. Like, that's what everyone says, because you've got a *mortgage* and *kids* and you're knee-deep in your *career* and there's just limited time, right?"

I need another bump.

"Well, no mortgage," Ndella says, her fingers splayed out, "and no kids. We're not doing too badly!" She laughs with gusto.

"Not in this financial climate," Alice says seriously, but she receives a few laughs. I do love the fact that Alice doesn't realise how

funny she is. I wish I could laugh about it too. I wish I could just pretend as if everything were normal. I almost wish I could rewind and the six of us would be sitting in halls – Darsh, Ndella, Alice, Doug, Christina and I – sipping Hooch, eating a Burns Night meal courtesy of Lidl. Sucking on a doobie.
My head starts to spin.

"Would you guys ever have kids?" I ask. Like I even *care*. These people are so boring it feels almost illegal. I don't know why I agreed to this over drinks with Claudia and the rest of the work lot. God, I think I'd rather *be* at work than listen to this dreary bullshit.

"Again, not financially viable," Alice says with a tinkly laugh. Her girlfriend is looking at her like she's in *a lot* of pain but is trying to conceal it. Shit, they've probably had this conversation a billion times. Whoopsie.

"We're actually trying for a baby," says the one who looks like Diana Silvers.
Ndella and Alice gasp and their weird, patronising friend slams his glass down on the table.

"I had no idea!" Alice says. Well, why the heck would you? These people are all the same – they just say things for the sake of it. I know *I've* been asking a lot of questions, but I'm trying to make the effort for Darsh's sake.

Doesn't really seem like his kind of crowd, though. I can't imagine him at uni with two lesbians, an alcoholic and a man who is clearly lacking in social skills. What's his name again? I can't even remember, that's how little he's contributed to any conversation.

"Good luck with it," Darsh says, raising his glass. He's so fucking cute. Our babies would be literally beautiful. Asian and white kids are always beautiful.

"Yeah, what an exciting journey!" Alice croons.

Then it all gets seriously fucking awkward.

"Why the hell," begins their weird friend, "are we talking about babies and finances when our friend is literally lying six feet under?"

The whole table goes silent. For a second I think he's just making like, another weird, sarcastic comment but when I look at Alice and Ndella they've gone rigid and Alice's face is as pale as a sheet of paper.

"We're sitting here sipping on poncy wine and admiring these cutesy fucking candles when Christina is…is…is…is fucking *dead*. And I don't know who the hell these two are…" he swings his glass in mine and Jen's direction, "…but I don't know why the fuck they're here when Doug is on medication for clinical *depression*. Just look at him!"

Doug is still staring at his plate, but his face is crumpling and he's rocking ever so slightly back and forth. Surely…?

"You think we can just sit here and eat potatoes whilst Christina's just rotting in the-"

"THAT'S ENOUGH," Ndella says, her voice so loud and firm that it pushes her out of her seat. Her bottom lip is trembling. My appetite, by this point, is completely gone. I feel *awful*. I knew there was something up with Doug. Not that I know the guy, but no-one has that glaze over their eyes unless they've really been through something.

"I'm just gonna…" Cindy is up and gesturing towards the front door. She grabs her bag and is gone in less than thirty seconds. Ndella's face is like thunder, but Alice has started to cry, her delicate blue eyes rimmed with red. Poor Alice. And poor, *poor* Doug. What an awful thing to say at a dinner party. What an awful thing to *happen* to someone so young. I don't know what to say. I don't *think* I should say anything – it's not my place to, yet the silence is so stifling. Alice just sits there crying, and Doug just sits there shaking his head, and Crew starts pacing round the room, his hands in his hair.

"Doug," says Ndella, and her voice is also

thick with tears that I think she's trying to hold in. "I'm really happy you came this evening. Alice wanted us to do something really nice. We wanted you to have an evening where, maybe, you didn't have to thi...where you didn't have to do all the things that I know are difficult to do right now-"

"Like sit here and listen to fucking small talk!"

Crew's voice is like the knife that just keeps thrusting. Poor Ndella is only trying to say the right thing, to take one for the team, because no-one else is able to. They just continue to look down at their plates, and I do the same.

Doug reaches across the table and takes Ndella's hand in his. She leans over and brings it up to her face and kisses it, finally releasing the tears. I find myself tearing up, too.

Darsh hasn't moved at all. Crew is the only one moving abruptly, and I can hear him sobbing now. I find myself standing up, though I don't think anyone notices. I find myself walking across to him and pulling him into a hug, and he leans against my chest, sobbing like a child. I've never heard a grown man cry like this before. Selfishly, I envision my future son. I don't mean to, but that's what springs to mind. He'll be tall like his dad, and maybe he will lean against my chest one day, heaving with sobs. Twenty, maybe even thirty years into the future. It's not that I'm trying to cling onto my own happiness, but this is the only way I can do something to help. I can't relate with what has happened to Crew, or any of them, especially Doug. This is the only way to show solidarity – to feel something that is important.

*His knife see Rustic-labour dicht*
*An' cut you up wi' ready slicht,*
*Trenching your gushing entrails bricht*
*Like onie ditch;*
*And then, Oh what a glorious sicht*
*Warm-reekin, rich!*

# HEINZ BAKED BEANS

Back in the kitchen. A low *grumble grumble grumble* – yes, yes, something's coming, don't *worry*, and yet the fridge has never been in a more sorrowful state, the freezer even worse: bare, barren, desolate, gaping, mouth a gaping hole, indignant. *There will be something*. The cupboards never disappoint – well, on this occasion, suffice it to say that

Heinz Baked Beans

are not exactly welcomed. Perched, slightly forlorn, the teal sleeve winking. Luckily – yes! – there is bread somewhere; what a pairing, *not all is lost*, apart from the zeal and excitement of embarking on a gastronomic adventure, a metamorphosis from tinned this and that to Whole Foods every weekend, inspired by the arrival of a new year. It should have started today, but with

*Heinz Baked Beans*

there is little to use creatively, nothing at all is gourmet about this sorry excuse for a meal, even the bread can't redeem it.
Sighing,
fling them into a bowl and into the microwave,
nothing at all is gourmet about this sorry excuse for a meal,
toast the bread,
butter the bread,
the beans go round and round,
nothing at all is gourmet about this sorry excuse for a meal,
crossed arms,
waiting,
nothing is gourmet about this-

and yet.

Little tin, teal sleeve winking, reticent globs that float about in the goo, plonked onto a supermarket shelf amid others (plenty of competition in these streets) but it's always,

always Heinz. Branston *Schmanston*.
Little tins,
big tins,
three-packs,
containers,
microwavable snappity pots – all part of a growing EMPIRE, a legacy left by none other than

Henry Heinz

Young, excited, Land of the Free's very own poster boy. Now we're ZOOMING across the Atlantic at full speed, or rather, chugging along at a steady speed, a ship with crates like boulders which – funnily enough – you could use as inspiration at dinnertime when you tip the tin and the beans come cascading over the toast, an avalanche of orange. Just as inevitably as said avalanche, the beans are a hit at upmarket department store Fortnum & Mason (if you're looking to sell anywhere it *has* to be here.) One taste of the sapid slop and the shop said

"We'll take the lot!"

Suddenly, *Heinz Baked Beans* are being sold at London's answer to Bloomingdale's. AND IT'S POSH NOSH! A New England tradition

– soon to be an English tradition. Fifteen years come and go and then

BAM!

The beans are being scattered across England, tins are reaching the richest and the poorest citizens, infiltrating the social stratosphere – why, EVEN THE QUEEN'S GORGING HERSELF SILLY! The factory doors are swinging open somewhere in the British heartlands – followed by a second set of doors elsewhere, and then another, and then another, because the public are enamoured, and by the roaring '20s they're HEINZ CRAZY!

(They even make it all the way to Antarctica – because how on earth can Robert Falcon Scott and his crew survive the perilous expedition without glacial gloops?)

The factories are chugging out 10,000 tonnes of grub and approximately A TRILLION humble beans are reaching dinner tables every day, but probably more. It's a BEAN-FEST, it's a SPECTACLE, a gaping hole in the market that, frankly, nobody knew existed, has been filled and now a full English without the fiery hue of tomatoey goodness is a travesty,

laughable,
sad.

BUT THEY'RE MUTATING!

The once sweet, saucy beans are being stripped of their molasses, and suddenly war has broken out, so WE CAN'T HAVE PORK NO MORE, BOYS! Time for…

RATIONING!

(Don't be disheartened, though – yes, people are dying but the Ministry of Food have classified *Heinz Baked Beans* as essential food, and so now they're exempt from any limitations. No sausage, but we can live with that – and by Jove, we're living!

THE COMPETITION

arrives and is, apparently, here to stay. The loyalists turn their noses up at the sight of decoy beans arriving faster than you can say 'put the kettle on', but there are plenty who are indifferent, satisfied with anything that looks squishy, slightly oblong and fluorescent pumpkin-coloured. But guess what?

*Beanz Meanz Heinz*

and if that doesn't clear things up for you, then I don't know what will.

So now we're at the TIPPITY TOP OF THE SINGLE MARKET, we're REACHING ABOVE THE CLOUDS, we're looking down at the BEAN EMPIRE, the BEANDOM, teal sleeves being tossed across oceans to reach SIXTY COUNTRIES that simply can't get enough, and now we begin our descent, PLUMMETING back down to the ground, SWOOPING across rooftops and grazing the tops of trees, FORKS CLATTERING about on plates as they SCRAPE UP the remains of beans on toast, we're SOMERSAULTING through windows until a crash into the kitchen counter where

the forlorn tin sits.

Or maybe it's not so forlorn, maybe it's standing, proud, surveying its kingdom, smug. After all, when all else fails, one simply can't go wrong with

*Heinz Baked Beans*

The microwave pings.

Inside the bowl, the once-clammy beans are bursting.

# WHEN I GROW UP

The pain is hot, like a knife's been in the oven and now it's slicing through flesh, or something. It feels like she's had a bowling pin shoved up there, knocking against her pelvic bone, and her insides are twisting and spasming in protest. She instantly tenses, which of course makes everything worse; her instinct is to push the sweaty, heavy mass of the boy away but then she remembers where she is and she has to fucking pull it together because it's getting embarrassing. He pulls out yet again and she feels like her bits have been in the frying pan (she hates using the word 'bits' but it can't be any worse than 'pussy', which is what most people say.) It feels like hot jelly down there, and her face crumples at the thought of it never, ever again being how it was before, a neat little package. She pulls herself together. She can't make it any more embarrassing, no, no and no.

"You need to relax," the boy mumbles.

Catrin suddenly decides how she can salvage this.

"Why don't you lie down?" It's meant to sound sexy and dominating but it comes out as a tentative suggestion, more sugar than spice. The boy looks down.

"Oh shit, you're bleeding."

He has a knack of stating the obvious, it seems. Catrin tries her very best to ignore the sopping mess between her goose-pimpled thighs and forces the boy to recline, hair swinging about her face, her lips chapped. Here is the distinguishable scent of sex, and it makes Catrin feel greasy but also stunned, like her childhood has been snatched out of her hands. Here is adulthood, apparently, and it looks like messy, flabby skin and the alarming blackness of pubic hair that smells like ham. She wonders how long it will take to actually have the desire to do this with somebody. The boy's dick (again, no words sound even slightly complimentary) is the colour of salmon and has globules of her own blood hugging the tip. Catrin already feels the urge to gag, and there's nothing in her mouth yet. There's no time to dither otherwise he will think she doesn't know what she's doing. It's cold up here.

Catrin knew it was normal to start thinking about the boy in *that* way, but she faced ambivalence daily, kind of like when she spent so long convincing herself she hated physics only to find that she got a kick out of unscrambling equations. She didn't act upon it straightaway, *obviously*. It was more a case of taking a new interest in watching films with naked actors, and sitting in her bedroom with no clothes on, pretending her hands were a boy's hands. Inevitably it never works despite the mental gymnastics you put yourself through trying to sever your nerve endings. But Catrin started to realise that eventually the body she had seen transform over the course of fifteen years didn't necessarily just have to be for her. Or, rather, it was something comforting and homely when it was just her and the mirror, but with someone else it had the potential to be something delectable.

Her friends talked about it. Or, rather, made predictions based on other people's experiences.

"Apparently you're supposed to drink cranberry juice to make yourself taste better."

"Taste better?"

"Yeah. You know, when he's eating you out."

Eating You Out. Catrin tried to process this. Not eating out with you, not wining and dining, but

Eating. You. Out. Catrin imagined an alien crunching through her insides and emerging through the gaping hole of her mouth.

"Your face is priceless, Cat."

"I mean," said Catrin, "doesn't it just taste like…I don't know, pee?"

"Do you not use toilet paper or something?"

"Obviously," said Catrin, indignant. "I mean, don't you just taste of, like…"

Like what exactly? Sometimes Catrin cupped a hand over her mouth to smell her own breath. She wanted to find another word but – ah – there it was…the inevitable disgust rising up, reminding her she was still a child, and maybe if she couldn't process this idea then maybe that was her cue to stay well clear.

"Pineapple juice does that, too, you know."

"I heard that everyone has a different taste."

"Some boys don't like doing it."

"Well, I'd rather not suck a dick, but it is what it is."

"What if the boy doesn't want to do it? How do you convince him that it's a good idea?"

"Tell him it feels good. And if he knows you enjoy it, he'll want to do it, trust me."

"What if I don't enjoy it?"

"All girls enjoy it, idiot."

"If you're so curious, you should talk to Lolly about it."

"Yeah, she knows everything, the slag. Take

her some sweets. She likes American Hard Gums and Pear Drops the best."

Catrin went into the girls' bathroom on the first floor during lunchbreak. She saw Lolly standing underneath the single window that no girl was tall enough to reach, and which served no purpose as the bathroom was always awash with the constant, cloying scent of cheap perfume and body spray. She stood under the window, her hair tousled and large, full of all the secrets she kept. Unbothered, she frantically ground down the same stick of chewing gum, acrylic nails tap-tap-tapping whilst she texted. Catrin stood in the doorway, wondering how to approach Lolly. There were far too many girls inside the bathroom currently for her to initiate conversation. Promptly she entered a cubicle and waited far too long for the bathroom to be cleared of voices. She plucked the offerings from her jacket and held them out to Lolly. Lolly stowed away her mobile phone and took the sweets.

"Whaddya wanna know?"

"Um…" began Catrin. "Um, basically, I want to…"

"Fuck your boyfriend?"

Catrin felt as if she'd caught her finger in the door. She looped her hands through the straps of her rucksack.

"Like, is the whole thing pretty straightforward?"

Catrin's heart was pounding. Lolly blew a sizeable bubble with her gum.

"It's kind of obvious what you do, right?" said Lolly, after the bubble had popped. "You know what goes where. I don't need to tell you that, you learn it at school for free, right? Just touch each other a lot. The more you touch each other, the more turned on you get. It's not gonna work if he's not hard and you're not wet. He's gonna be better at jacking himself off, just as you're gonna know how to touch yourself. The one thing he can't do is give himself a blowjob, obviously, so you're gonna want to do that, so that he'll go down on you in return. I can show you how to give a good blowjob, but it'll be two packets of strawberry bonbons, and maybe a jawbreaker." Lolly stuck her hand out.

Catrin considered this for several seconds. Then she shook her head.

"No, it's okay, thanks. But what if he doesn't want to eat me? Out?"

She had left it just a millisecond too long before adding the final word, and Catrin's face flushed. Lolly shifted in her spot and carefully realigned her right eyelash strip.

"Like I already said, if you give him a blowjob, he'll return the favour. That's always worked for me."

"And what if he doesn't?"

Lolly stopped chewing abruptly.

"You're obviously doing something wrong."

The boy doesn't go down on her even after she's spent fifteen minutes trying not to gag, the tears stinging her eyes. He says it's because she's bleeding, so Catrin tactfully removes herself from the room to go and shower. The harsh light of the bathroom highlights the weird black hairs that have started protruding from her nipples and the aqua veins of her thick thighs, and Catrin lets the water wash away the gamy smell of sex. She moves a hand between her legs and the watery blood is like a splash of paint. She opens her mouth and lets the warm water rise, realising, with disillusionment, that there is, of course, a distinctive taste emanating from the body's intimate, porous landmarks. Her face flares up at the recollection of all that gooey, milky *slop* and its putrid smell and she wants to scrub her skin with as much exertion as possible because she feels sick to her stomach now, and the only thing she really wants to swallow her is the ground, so she doesn't have to go back into the bedroom and face the boy. He's probably messaging his friends to tell them what a tedious experience he's just had, and she'll return to find him staring at the TV screen with his thumbs straining at the console, knee-deep in dead bodies while she's been scooping up the fallen soldiers from her own body. She watches the smear of blood vanish with the weight of the pounding rain of the showerhead. Maybe it wasn't blood after all, but cranberry juice; she sure drank enough of the stuff. The boy obviously wasn't aware of this whole juice strategy, because all Catrin could taste was battery acid, to put it nicely.

Vodka and cranberry juice are a surprisingly decent combination. Maybe it's not so surprising – for such a small berry, cranberry has a potent, sour flavour that pretty much overrides the taste of anything else, even paint stripper. But Catrin can still taste the vodka; here is a new world in the form of societies and ten-thousand-word documents and fluorescent liquids opening its doors, where everything is akin to a slap in the face. There is no preparation; she is thrust into it – and now she must dance, wildly, with little rhythm. In the SU, her chartreuse t-shirt sticking to her back, Catrin is confronted with the realisation that she is stuck with these new faces, who are all bubbly and well-meaning and excitable, for the next year.

Every Wednesday, Friday and Saturday Catrin dons various forms of ridiculous dress and plays shot roulette with these new people, though each night there are newcomers who drift in and out, visitors, fellow students with tenuous links to Catrin's flatmates. She has some of the most intimate conversations with these stragglers, who then disappear, whose faces Catrin wouldn't be able to pick out in a crowd seven days later. But then one Wednesday she meets Guy, and this is a face she knows she won't be able to forget in a hurry.

When Catrin looks back at that night she is overcome by a delicious feeling. How satisfying it is to remember being on one side of the room, casting occasional glances at the dark and handsome stranger, and then fast-forwarding to the two of them gyrating on the dancefloor, and then fast-forwarding again to Catrin touching Guy where only a handful of others have touched him before. When she saw him, it had awoken something primal in her that had been lying dormant, but at the same time she wanted to stroke his hair tenderly. This was not how she had felt before. This was new, different. He looked older than most of the fresh-faced eighteen-year-olds in the room – herself included – and there was also something beautiful about the way he held the glass. Catrin didn't realise men could be beautiful too, but here was a first glimpse into yet another world. There weren't fireworks when she kissed Guy – it was more of a jolt that ran from Catrin's belly button down to her pussy (surely there must be a less crude word, somewhere, *somewhere*.) The next thing Catrin knew she was lying in bed with him, and she didn't feel like a girl having sex, but a woman just doing a Normal Thing. Thus began the start of something, a narrative in which Guy would come to her at night, mostly after he'd been out on the town, usually when Catrin was also intoxicated. It's still not the fireworks that Catrin has been waiting for, but it's okay; mostly she just feels good about being wanted.

"I'm great at this, trust me," Guy says to her, moving himself further down the bed until she can only see his hair and his arms with all the dark fluff. This is the first time Guy has ventured down there, and when Catrin doesn't feel the euphoria she had expected to knock her out, she hears words from a distant time in her head and wonders if this is what it's like being a plastic bag. Not like the plastic bag in *American Beauty*, no, but empty and flat. Now she's exasperated because she's thinking about plastic bags, is not even present in the bedroom while Guy is doing a lot of complicated things with his tongue, and this makes it even harder to think about how to get something, *anything*, out of being Eaten Out. When Guy comes up for air with a boyish grin, he seems so pure that Catrin cannot be mad about anything, not really, and she kind of wishes that maybe one time they could Eat Out (instead.) Even just Nando's would be fine with her. And in this moment, right here, she just kind of wants to lie entwined in his arms until she falls asleep, but then he will leave and she will be left with the feeling of ambivalence that lingers and distracts her from everything she does. And Catrin wonders if that's a normal thing, too.

"I don't even like coffee," Catrin's friend says.
Everyone drinks coffee, that and alcohol. These are more Normal Things. Different liquids serve different purposes. This is something Catrin discovered within her first week of being at university, as well as the fact that adults (real adults) do not check up on you, and that there are people who do not know that pasta needs to be boiled in hot water.
Catrin doesn't particularly like the taste of coffee either but she grins and bears it, until she sees Guy enter the SU and the taste of bitter liquid becomes even more pungent, so much so that it takes every fiber of her being not to spit it out, a slow blush creeping up her neck onto the bare skin of her face because she decided, today of all days, to stay on campus looking simultaneously haggard and like a twelve-year-old, leggings and duffel coat the outfit of choice. She's stunned for a moment because he's

caressing the girl's hands, and she looks from the girl to Guy, her eyes unable to focus for more than a second because she's finding it hard to process what is actually happening, and Catrin's friend is still chattering away but then she stops and says, "oh" in an uneven voice which confirms that yes, this is bad, very bad, and Catrin stands up to go to the bathroom because she has to escape, now, immediately, even if he's already seen her.

The bathroom is a haven. Catrin, already feeling like the epitome of the word pathetic, quickly realises how much she loves the girls' bathroom, and, in fact, it just might be the best place in the world. It's private and there are no men and though it's not homely like a bedroom, it doesn't *have* a bed to remind you that you're alone at night or that you spent so many times with a person who doesn't care in the slightest about your feelings, and in fact was just using you as something he could chew and spit back out again. The bathroom, with its fluorescent lights and quiet hum of running water and, controversially, its blasting of the hand-dryer, is a soothing place. Catrin has enjoyed the bathrooms at uni, especially on nights out, because although girls are throwing up and making out and crying, they can be wholly themselves, and they say lovely, uplifting, wonderful things to each other, including Catrin.

Catrin stops shaking eventually. When she and her friend come out of the bathroom, Guy and the girl are gone, but the air has changed. When he doesn't text her and she doesn't text him, Catrin wonders if he *did* see her. All she knows (via the nosy girl from two floors down) is that this is the first time Guy's girlfriend has visited him on campus, a fact that hurls itself at Catrin with as much force as an asteroid and sends her into an apathetic state for several days. When she is ready Catrin doesn't so much emerge from it as violently crashes out of it. She eats her first proper meal and vomits all over the kitchen floor. She had been imagining Guy inside his girlfriend, his face pressed up against her vulva, his mouth smashed against hers, and then had been imagining him doing the same to Catrin. Catrin runs to the bathroom to clean her teeth. If she keeps thinking about fragments of the girl's DNA lingering somewhere in her own body, she will surely heave again, and there's no way she's recording that on the flat's chunder chart.

"Single or double?"
"Double."
Catrin pours.
"Actually, do you have any cranberry juice?" Catrin is immediately taken back to university, back to the feeling of her teeth rotting whilst

chugging back drinks in the artificial light of the industrial campus kitchens. She looks at the eager punter and wonders if one day she will prefer pomegranate molasses to Ocean Spray or San Pellegrino to Sainsbury's Basics lemonade. Maybe this butterfly woman *is* really only twenty-one like it says on her ID (everybody looks older these days) and her small-town life revolves around Wetherspoons and shopping on the high street, driving six miles for a decent meal. Maybe she's come to the city for her best friend's birthday party and the Be At One a few streets away was full, so here she is, full face of make-up slightly greyish under the harsh lights and a tell-tale streak of fake tan on her left shoulder, needing sugar, sugar and more sugar.

Catrin fixes her the drink, takes the payment and then moves on to the next, butterfly woman fading into the crowd forever. Catrin doesn't mind working in the bar. She gets to make up profiles for each punter whilst juggling various ingredients, and surely that must be a skill? Not that she needs to justify her career choices – it's mindless labour she needs, she craves. It's funny being on the other side – back at university (what a drag, thank God she scraped through) life was blurred and the headaches were…well, harrowing. Now Catrin gets to deal with the slurred speech and the toe-curling screams sober, and it's funny at best and at worst fucking awful. For this very reason, she does sometimes indulge in a drink or two. But she also gets to slink off to the bathroom whenever she needs to, her haven, the place where she can just sit and breathe. Sometimes she just takes a seat and pretends that she's giving out extra toilet roll. The girls stagger in, pissing and shitting and throwing up their guts, cleansing themselves – it's a satisfying process for Catrin and she enjoys it. Perhaps enjoy is too strong a word, but she really doesn't mind it at all.

"Catrin?"

Catrin looks up. Cue significant encounter numéro trois, the clean-shaven man with neat, slicked hair. It's his skin. His skin is smooth, porcelain, completely hairless and he's tall, but not in an aggressive, intimidating way.

"I'm sorry, have we met?"

"No – I'd remember."

Catrin realises she is wearing a name badge and grins sheepishly. The man is smiling back at her, and suddenly it rears its head – that carnal feeling. It takes her by surprise.

"What are you drinking?" Catrin asks.

"An espresso martini, if you'd be so kind."

A cocktail drinker. A strategic man – two vices rolled into one, caffeine and alcohol. Catrin never really got into coffee. Her colleagues tease her about having such a sweet tooth, making her out to be a child, because apparently only children eat sweets and drink juice and consume the most delicious things life has to offer. She stands by her choices, regardless of what they say.

Catrin stands by her choice to sleep with the man even though he tells her he's slept with other women. This is what she had feared, but she must deal with it.

"Is that a problem?" he asks with bemusement. "Are you a purist or religious or something?"

"No, I'm…no," Catrin says. "Do you mind taking a shower though?"

"Are you joining me?" he grins.

"No, I've showered today already. Do you mind brushing your teeth, too? I'm just not a fan of coffee."

The man, nonplussed, obliges. As he trails kisses down her neck and onto her breasts, tongue swirling around the nipples, Catrin tries hard not to think about the other women, their skin slick with saliva and other fluids. She stops the man from going any further south and instead straddles him. There is no climax for her, and she removes herself before he comes, watching as his gleaming body writhes and shudders. Catrin feels her perspiration and runs to the bathroom before he's finished twitching.

The next and final person has never done the deed, and this is euphoric for Catrin. When he touches her, she feels something of a sugar rush, and she has prepared well for the occasion, having lathered herself in body butter that smells like passionfruit. She still made him shower, but asked if he could put his clothes back on so she could undress him herself. Peeling the clothes off him, Catrin observes his skin, pale and soft like fruit. He is not particularly muscular but she'd rather less hair than muscles – she wants smooth, glossy, unchartered territory.

The man, when he isn't entwined in Catrin's arms, has a good job, something related to physics. Perhaps Catrin would have gone down the same route had she been motivated enough.

"But you're happy at the bar?" he asks Catrin over dinner. They are poring through the menu. It's a fancy restaurant, one she'd never stepped foot in before, and because he insists on paying Catrin must make a wise decision.

"Yeah," she says, distracted. "I'm thinking oysters. We may as well!" She flashes him a smile. They're also full of zinc, perfect for helping the body make testosterone.

"Nice choice!" he says. "You're right, we may as well. Wine? There's a delicious white

that I think would go perf-"
Catrin has scrunched up her face.

"I'm indifferent, but you do your thing," she says. She still saves the alcohol for the hard times which, luckily, have presented themselves less and less these days. This man has made sure of that, and she is grateful.

"Thank you, Chip," she says, squeezing his hand.

"I still don't know where you plucked that nickname from, and I thought I'd hate it, but I like it," says Chip, shaking his head and grinning.

"It's just better than Baby or Cutie Pie or Honey or any of that other crap," Catrin says, rolling her eyes.

The waiter takes their orders.

"I'll also have whatever juice you've got," Catrin tells him, handing the menu over.

Catrin has never been able to hold a man's attention for longer than a few months, but for some reason, Biscuit is enamoured with her. This is unchartered territory. Despite that, she finds it all surprisingly easy. She gets up early, makes him breakfast before he goes to work (lots of fruit and avocado) makes him dinner (usually fish) and then trots off to the bar. She takes lead of the shopping and cooking, has found that domesticated life suits her very well indeed. Chip enjoys her cooking, enjoys her company, enjoys her body.

"But why won't you let me go down on you?" he asks, tracing her belly button with his finger.

"Because I don't really like it," Catrin replies, which isn't entirely untrue. He asks her every time they have sex, and her answer is always the same.

"But maybe you just haven't had anyone who knows what they're doing," Chip counters. He says this every time, too.

"If I fancy it, I'll let you know."
Catrin kisses him. A small part of her is suddenly terrified that he will lose interest in her because of this, but then she quashes this thought, knowing full well that he is far too wrapped up in his own pleasure to ever want to do this. She finds herself compensating all the same, going above and beyond to satisfy him, and when they both have time off work, they lie naked in each other's arms for hours on end, perhaps days.

"You need to shave," she says, holding him by the chin.

They are having fish again. Chip smiles at her, but something is off – she can tell. She spends so long looking at his face that she knows every minute detail, every twitch of the eyebrow and twist of the mouth.

"What is it?"

"Nothing!" he says, overly enthusiastic.

Catrin puts her cutlery down.

"You're a terrible liar."

"*Babe.*"

He chews, probably biding his time. Catrin watches him.

"You know I love everything you make," he says. The 'but' hangs in the air in front of them enticingly.

Catrin takes a swig of her juice.

"You know, it's Friday, you're not working for once, I'm not working because it's the end of the week, we've got a night in – maybe we should have had a takeaway or something? We never do that."

"Huh," says Catrin. She doesn't speak for a moment. "You know, I'm not really a massive fan of-"

"Junk food, I know," Chip says, smiling. "You say that, but I think you're just trying to be, I don't know, overly healthy. You can cut yourself some slack, you know. You've gotta live."

"I do live," Catrin says, frowning. "Since when does eating crap equal a fulfilled life? I'm just happy with what I do, what I eat. That's all." She doesn't need to be angry at him. He's just, understandably, wanting to be a good boyfriend, to mix things up, to show he's what, concerned about her? He doesn't need to be. At least she's not addicted to fried chicken, or an alcoholic, or obese. There are many, many things worse than actually *liking* healthy food. And sure, Catrin has her own vices – sweet things, for one. She loves sweet things, always has, always will. She doesn't tell *him* how to live his life, so why should he make assumptions about her? How *dare* he be so judgmental.

Catrin stands up abruptly.

"Hey, I'm sorry," says Chip.

"I'm just going to the toilet," she mumbles.

She sometimes makes lunch for Chip, but most of the time he buys lunch when he's at work, which distresses her. She's been finding beef jerky wrappers in the bin, been noticing Chip use dairy milk for tea when they switched to oat months ago, was concerned when he came back from a mate's having inhaled an entire, gargantuan pizza and half a loaf of garlic bread all to himself. She couldn't touch him that night, refused his advances between the sheets, facing the other way and staring into the dark, burying her face into the satin pillowcase that she sprayed with essential oils. He even tried again in the morning, though he knows she despises morning sex, can't even bear to kiss his mouth when it hasn't been cleaned for eight hours. At work she drinks more than usual, mixing random ingredients to try out new cocktails. She remembers when she first tried alcohol, during that heady, clamorous first week at uni, noticed the way it turned even the calmest and quietest of students into revolutionary versions of themselves. The possibilities were endless for the inebriated – they felt they could do anything. Was it not alcohol that cajoled her into walking up to Guy and dancing with him in the SU? Was it not that mysterious substance that pushed her to reach up and kiss his lips hungrily? She couldn't even taste whatever unappealing acidity coated his mouth because the alcohol had masked that too, that and her shyness and all the other things that maybe she wanted to repress. She never succumbed to it, though. And she watches the punters stagger about, their limbs flailing this way and that, like they've got some kind of fungal infection, except its alcohol overseeing the operation, spurning them on to do ridiculous things that they'd never do sober.

Chip is far from sober.
She hasn't seen him this drunk before, but here he is, staggering through the house like a foal unsure of its own legs, unable to even find the light switch. How *stupid*. She stands in the dark, watching him until he notices her and then

pauses, swaying slightly.

"Babe, I'm fucked," he mumbles. Men really do have a knack of stating the obvious, it seems.

"Why did you drink so much?" she asks him, her voice giving away nothing. He takes a breath, ready to make a sarcastic comment, but is unable to gather the strength or enough brain cells to do so. Instead, he settles for: "How's your night been?" He is grinning at her.

"Not great, because I've been worrying about you," Catrin says. "I thought you said you'd be back by midnight."

"What if I didn't *want* to be back by midnight?" he replies sharply, a petulant child, throwing his hands out. "What if I just got a bit *carried away?* It happens, you know."

He swaggers over to the sink to grab himself a glass of water, even though there's filtered water in the fridge but no matter, he always fucking forgets about that.

"You're going to feel like shit tomorrow," Catrin says.

"Maybe I already feel like shit!" He slams the glass down on the countertop, making Catrin jump.

"There's no need to shout," she says quietly.

"Well, you know what? Sometimes you really give me something to shout about, Catrin. Can you stop fucking…watching me like that?"

Catrin stays put, reeling slightly from all the swearing. Chip never swears. She's never heard him say a foul thing about anybody.

"Why do you already feel like shit?" she asks.

"Because…" He trails off. "It's…" He slaps the kitchen counter. "No, fuck it, I'm gonna say it. It's *getting* to me now, Cat, all this 'don't eat this, don't eat that, take this, take that, be back by this time, drink enough water, maybe don't touch that, what's this I've found?' and blah, blah, blah. I've always been patient." He turns around to face her, gesturing with his hands, calming himself. Then he belches. "I've always been tolerant. But now…I don't know, it's *too much,* Cat. It's taking a toll on me. You make me feel like shit. I don't know how else to say it.

Catrin is quiet.

"I love you, you know," Chip says.

Catrin puts her head in her hands, then straightens up, releasing a long moan as she does so.

"No, no, *no,* Chip. I don't want you to tell me that now, whilst you're drunk and having a go at me. That's not…why would you do that?"

"Oh, for god's sake, Cat, it's the truth. I love you even though you're crazy sometimes."

"How am I crazy?" she shouts, and then she slumps, the point proven, defeated, frustrated, *angry*, out of control. Things were so good. For the first time in her life, she's felt like she's had something good, a man who hasn't abandoned her, who cherishes her, who does what she wants. But no, deep down he's not happy. What the fuck is wrong with them? So easy to please in bed, so fucking difficult to please in any other context.

This soft man. This handsome man with his smooth skin and his sweet words and his clean mouth; she's sure she could bite him and nothing but honey would pour out from the wound, but now he's angry – his eyes are dark, stormy – and she wants to know what has to give.

"I think – and I mean this in the nicest possible way, Cat – I think you have a problem," Chip says, even though she wants, *needs* him to stop talking, right now. "I'm not some kind of contaminated human being that you can just…I'm so *open* with you, I go above and beyond for you. And what do you do in return? You close yourself off. You act like some sort of beacon of piety…"

He carries on but she's not listening. It's over. It has to be.

"Fuck you," she growls.

"Don't do that, Cat. Hear me out-"

"No, I don't want to. Get out."

He pauses.

"I'm not going anywhere-"

"I said, *get out*," She is speaking slowly. "I'm done. I've been thinking about this for a while and I'm done. Please. Please just get out." They are face-to-face. Chip grimaces, turning away from her, shaking his head in disbelief or defeat, Catrin isn't sure.

"Fine," he says, "but don't you dare pretend that I was never good enough for you." He starts walking away from her.

The kitchen is silent but the noise in Catrin's head is deafening. She can't help relaying the conversation over and over, wishing he had never mentioned feeling contaminated or that she treated him as such, like he was flawed or tainted, because he *wasn't,* he was soft and smooth and sweet and clean and when they had sex he didn't disgust her, she was met with a delicious feeling each and every time, and he'd never known anybody else but also…he'd never known anybody else, and she had, and *God, did she wish* she could erase the past, the blood and the sweat and the tears and however many women had come before her and had touched the same hands and kissed the same lips and whatever else. Catrin is bending over the counter now, looking inwards; Biscuit never said a bad word about her, but she was not like him, not perfect, if anything *she* was the contaminated one, and no amount of showering or brushing could ever disguise that. She hasn't been to the dentist in years. She looks into the sink, at her reflection, grimaces, baring teeth, tasting that familiar taste, her mouth flooding with saliva, her stomach gurgling, and then she's heaving. The pain is dull, like a jawbreaker sitting at the bottom of her stomach, lolling to one side and pressing against her.

# BIRTH(DAY)

For my tenth birthday I received a beautiful, hand-crafted dolls house from my father. It had a blush-pink roof, Georgian windows and it was the best present I had ever been given. It was the last thing my father ever did for me, because days later he packed his bags and left. I still have the dolls house – I'd like my daughter, Freya, to enjoy it when she's older – but I cannot admire it to the same degree anymore; instead, I view it with a sense of cool indifference, sometimes unease. I will never know whether my father was being genuine when he presented it to me all those years ago, or whether the house's photo-perfect exterior was designed to mock, silently thriving on schadenfreude as it watched our fatherless family tear each other to pieces.

Today I am ascending the steps to the pistachio-green front door of our own perfect Georgian townhouse in North London, Freya in tow. She is a month old and flawless. As I reach for the keys in my pocket I steal another glance at her tiny hands, pink as prawns, and the slithers of fingernails I cannot believe grew inside my own body. The pregnancy was, in a word, awful, but Freya is perfect. There is always relief that follows pain, and everyone says that the pain of pregnancy is something you forget.

Today is my husband Richard's birthday. Humming, we enter the house, and it is pristine. Julia has been, and I'm hoping to catch her before she leaves. I park the pram in the hallway and try the kitchen first. Empty. I wander through to the dining room, then the sitting-room. It's deathly quiet, which is rather unusual as Julia likes a singsong as she cleans. It's a shame she's tone-deaf, amongst other things. I didn't really want to let her go, but needs must. I'm sure she understands.

"Keren?"

Her voice catches me off guard and my heart bumps against my chest somewhat clumsily. Julia emerges from the dim confines of the downstairs toilet and smiles. For a second I can't remember whether or not I sent the e-mail and I hesitate, but then I return the smile, briefly, for this is an awkward matter.

"I appreciate this must be difficult for you…"

"It's okay," Julia stammers. "I understand."

Just as I was hoping.

"Well, look," I say, moving towards the pram and my handbag, which is stowed underneath Freya's sleeping frame, "you've done a lot for us, really, so…this is me saying thank you."

I pluck five notes from my purse and stretch my hand out towards Julia. A peace offering. Blushing, she accepts, and briefly counts the money before shaking her head.

"This is very generous, Keren."

"I know," I say.

There is a slight pause. Julia clears her throat, looks down at her scuffed shoes and then at me, her pretty eyes shining.

"Thank you," she says, and her voice is slightly hoarse. "I wish you all the best, Keren."

I nod gratefully.

"I've actually, er, been excited to get back to the housework," I lie. I'm not sure why I'm saying this. I'm not sure why I'm attempting to make conversation. I think it's because I'm not very good at being brusque or deliberately cold. It's not in my nature. And Julia has always been lovely – it's hard to imagine her being anything but courteous and kind.

She nods and smiles. I imagine she just wants to leave as soon as possible.

"Take care of yourself," I say, and I mean it. Julia nods and smiles once more, avoiding eye contact. She grabs the bag hanging on the coat rail and is out of the door before I can take off my shoes. The house is silent once again, slightly eerie. I shiver. It is growing dark, and I'm aware of shady thoughts creeping, the ones I'm pretty sure I managed to banish to the dark recesses of my mind.

I need a drink.

I take Freya to her cot. Sometimes I wonder if I'm slowly going mad because I struggle to leave her alone, even when I'm in the house. My sister told me that she was the same after her first. She said that it's to do with having had the baby inside of you for so long. The transition from being one body to being two distinct individuals can be difficult to deal with. It makes a lot of sense. I wonder how long I'll feel like this, though. Sometimes, just sometimes, I still feel traumatised by the whole ordeal, then I feel guilty for feeling traumatised. It's a bizarre cycle and Richard will never understand, which makes things harder because he is the one person to whom I want to express these things. He is the person who sees me every day – at my best and at my worst – after all.

In the kitchen, I fix myself a drink. Whisky – Yamazaki, on the rocks. Richard's favourite. It's his birthday, so I'm drinking to him.

Cooking tonight fills me with anticipation. I told Richard that I wanted to make him a nice meal, but he wasn't exactly jumping for joy at the news. He's got this idea that I still need to rest, that I need time to return to 'normal' – needless to say, he isn't all that comfortable with me cooking, or doing any sort of physical labour. I suppose I thought he was being sweet at first.

In truth, I haven't cooked very much since Freya was born, but that's not because I don't feel confident. Living with a food critic means that naturally my husband has a way with both words and ingredients – he takes the two and turns them into some kind of magic. That's probably how I fell for him, in hindsight. I turn on the oven.

Richard had a blog five years ago; he was trying to get himself out there. I was too, I suppose. When Richard got in contact to say he was heading to Cornwall with a freshly broken DSLR and in need of a Truro-based photographer for his weekend trip, I couldn't turn down the offer. I'd looked him up online and felt the heat rising in my neck as I studied his face. I envisioned us sampling south-west England's finest seafood, conversing over wine, long walks on the beach with ice-cream – and that's exactly what happened. It was as if I'd manifested it. He was incredibly funny and took his work seriously. It made me think that he'd take us seriously, I suppose.

I take another swig of whisky. There's a lot of cutting to be done. I took the meat out to defrost before I left the house, and it's sitting in a bowl, the studded crystals of ice running slowly like tears.

That was an idyllic trip, it really was. I packed my bags and moved to London with him two years later and haven't looked back since. Cornwall is a magical place if you treat it like a holiday, otherwise it's isolated, quiet, full of elderly people reminding you that death is never too far away. You can get stuck there, like my sister did with her sorry excuse for a husband, nothing for her to do except pop out child after child. She's the only one that lives there now; the rest of the family scattered as soon as they got the chance.

Richard loves lasagna almost as much as

he loves whisky. He tells me that there are very few things he could eat again and again, and lasagna is one of them. So, lasagna he shall have.

Maybe I should dress up, take him by surprise. That's another thing I haven't done much since before I got pregnant with Freya. As soon as I put our dinner in the oven, I check on her. She wakes up as I enter, suddenly ravenous. It's like she knew I was coming. It makes me smile, to know that we are still connected despite being detached. I take her to my bedroom and let her feed, gazing into my wardrobe as I perch on the edge of the bed, balloon breasts sagging. The dark circles are awful, really.

Richard texted to say he'd be home around half-past seven, and he arrives at half-past seven on the dot, face rosy with the glow of several pints. I'm in the dining room, dressed up, laying cutlery, singing to Freya as she reclines in the baby bouncer. Richard looks surprised. My heart surges.

"Wow," Richard says, a slow smile spreading across his face. "Very exciting."

"You don't know what we're having yet," I reply, and retreat to the kitchen to fetch the wine glasses.

"Well, it smells delicious. And you

look…different. Beautiful."

My heart surges again. Richard stops me in my tracks and plants a kiss on my cheek. I can feel the warmth radiating from him; he probably needs a shower. He's been at work since nine, and then to the pub. Quite the socialite.

"Freya's had a great day today," I tell him.

"Ah," says Richard, looking over to Freya as if seeing her for the first time. He approaches the baby bouncer and chucks her under the chin. I don't think he really knows how to handle our child yet. Parenting doesn't exactly come naturally to him. Richard treats babies and children like spices – he spends time trying to figure out what good they can do for him, where best they slot in. Sometimes he likes having them around and at other times, he deems them loud and unnecessary.

"Tell me about work," I say.

He joins me in the kitchen, and I watch as he moves around, loosening his shirt collar, recounting incidents of hate mail. He outlines the details of the Japanese small plates he had the pleasure of sampling at lunchtime whilst I take out a bottle of red from the wine cabinet.

"What have you made?" he asks me suddenly.

"Lasagna."

A smile spreads across his face. He darts over

to me and gently removes the bottle from my hand.

"In that case, let's have the Barbera."
I mishear him at first, then offer him a warm smile.

Freya's on the verge of falling asleep just at the right time, so I make a quick trip upstairs to the bedroom. I feed her once more before she drifts off, staining my carmine dress in the process. It's inevitable – my breasts leak so often, weeping like sores. It's not a pretty sight, and no matter how much make-up I put on or how much I dress up I am never quite sexy enough. To be honest, there's not much I can do about that. It's a little too late to be lamenting.

The table is prepared. I open the oven and bring out the steaming lasagna. It looks like the best dish I've ever made, and in that moment, I don't care about the impending critique from Richard about the cheese to tomato ratio, or the herb quantity, or whether the sheets of pasta are al dente enough for him. Right now, with the dish warming my gloved hands, I feel a keen sense of satisfaction, and am emboldened.

"Such a great wine," Richard says as I place the dish down on the dining-room table. His eyes dart over the food; his nose twitches.

He looks up at me, incredulous.

"Lord Jesus. I wonder where you learnt to cook like that," he says, taking a sip of wine.

I can't help smiling.

"Cheers." I raise my glass to his. They connect. I think about the way Richard hasn't so much as touched me in months, and we dig in.

The lasagna is good. Really good. I watch Richard carefully as he chews, and my mind turns to Freya, as usual. My nipples moisten. Richard has closed his eyes. This is a good sign.

"Happy Birthday," I say.

Richard opens his eyes and swallows.

"This," he says, "is beautiful, Keren. I feel like you've put your own spin on it. Why haven't you made lasagna before?"

"It's a special recipe."

"Special recipe?"

I nod, taking another bite. The meat is beefy and tender, rich and yet delicate.

"Well, compliments to the chef," Richard says, grinning. "What a day! Thirty-six, Keren. Do you think I look thirty-six?"

"I'd say more…thirty-seven."

He grins, mouth slick with cheese oil. In truth, he looks young for his age – despite the alcohol and the constant eating out. His face is smooth; there is an eerie absence of fine lines.

Maybe there's a secret spirulina smoothie he hasn't told me about.

"We've been married for three years," I declare, and his chewing slows, as if he's scared of what's coming next. "Married for three years, and I still don't know if there's anything you wouldn't eat."

Richard swallows and lets out a chuckle.

"Anything I wouldn't eat?" he echoes, brows furrowing. "Let's see...no, nothing springs to mind. Oh, apart from *sannakji*."

I wait for him to expand and, of course, he does.

"A Korean delicacy. Live octopuses, chopped up, their arms still moving. That's all you need to know."

"That's horrid."

"I know. Terribly cruel. There are some things you just don't do." He pops another small parcel of lasagna into his mouth. I'm starting to feel quite queasy. I take a swig of wine.

"What about you?" Richard asks.

"Not a fan of offal," I reply.

"Oh, you're missing *out*."

I wait until Richard has finished his meal, until his plate has been licked clean and he is sitting back in his chair with his glass of wine, looking like the happiest man in the world.

"Well," I say, placing my knife and fork

down carefully. "I know I said liver and black pudding and haggis and all that wasn't really for me, but believe it or not, placenta is pretty tasty."

Richard's eyebrows collide and he cocks his head to one side.

"Placenta?" he echoes. "I don't think I can get behind that. Wow. When did you…?"

"That's a shame, darling. I thought you'd be open to it," I reply.

All it takes is a moment of silence for him to realise. Then, all of a sudden, Richard stands up, the chair screeching as it scrapes against the wooden floor. His eyes bulge, his mouth is agape and I have the sudden urge to slam it shut, but there's no need – he's out of the room and retching elsewhere before I know it. My heart is hammering just as I anticipated, but I breathe slowly, trying to stay calm. I will not get emotional. I've done my share of crying and punching pillows.

Instead, I take a sip of wine.

Richard eventually returns to the room, wiping his mouth, trembling. He looms over me, hands on hips, trying to hold himself together – there's even the ghost of a smile on his face.

"Uh, Keren," he says. "You really should have fucking told me about this beforehand."

I take another sip of wine.

"Sit down."

He stares at me for a second, then obliges. Freya, my poor Freya, if only she were aware of the situation at hand. I hope I never have to recount this evening to her, not even when she's eighteen and wanting to know everything about the world.

Richard is starting to sweat.

"I guess now you know what it feels like to be gifted something you didn't ask for," I say. His eyebrows knit together.

"You think I didn't know? You think I'm really *that* oblivious, that giving birth to our daughter somehow messed with my head and now I can't work, cook, sleep with you, act like a rational human being? You're sorely mistaken, Richard."

"Keren," says Richard softly, "I'm afraid I'm lost. What is this about?"

"The women, Richard, the women."

"Which women?"

"The women you've been lusting after. Wanting to sleep with."

I wonder which facial expression Richard will settle for. He decides on a quiet chuckle, his eyes closed, his eyebrows raised.

"Keren, really? Are we really doing this?"

"Richard, I've just cooked you a lovely meal. How about you sit and listen to what I have to say? It's the least you can do."

"I'm not…I'm not going to fucking sit here and listen to you jump to some ridiculous conclusion, Keren." His voice has an edge to it. "I'm not going to give you the chance, I'm sorry."

"What are you going to do instead? Gag me? Walk away?"

He is gazing at me, almost disappointedly. Then he covers his face with his hands, leans back and laughs.

"All this cooking just so you can back me into corner and make wild accusations," he says bitterly. "Some birthday."

"You joke that I learnt to cook from the best," I say, "but I'm afraid I can't really say the same for you. I thought you'd have learnt, over the years, about photography. You know how much I love it, how much I talk about it. And yet you choose the cheapest digital camera you can get your hands on to take grotesque photos of women I can't even identify, and you *store* those photos in an empty peanut butter tub in your office." I laugh. "Perhaps it's not so reckless, because one thing you do know is how much I hate peanut butter. But Richard, pregnancy gives you the strangest cravings, it really does. I searched high and low for that peanut butter tub, convinced that you'd bought some weeks before, and I knew you wouldn't keep it in the kitchen because it was what you liked to snack on whilst typing at your desk. That's why it was so bizarre that I had to conduct an in-depth investigation into the whereabouts of this fucking peanut butter tub. You'd hidden it. And no wonder."

"Keren...look," Richard says, leaning forwards. "Okay. You found the photographs. But *believe* me – they're old. And I didn't take them myself, you've got to trust me on that. I was younger, I was stupid, horny, whatever you want to call it-"

"Then why do you still have them? And why did I have such a horrific conversation with a tearful Julia last week?"

"What did she say? Did *she* find the photos?" Richard looks exasperated, the sweat threatening to run down his face, which is flushed.

"No. She said that you've been making comments to her. Touching her inappropriately."

"Bullshit!"

"I thought so myself. I so wanted to believe she was lying. But it became such a regular occurrence that she came to expect it. That's why she took the voice recording."

Retrieving my phone from the sideboard, I played Richard the file Julia had sent me. Richard, his face as red as lobster, stands and begins to pace. I think he is crying but I can't tell if it's tears or sweat pouring down his face.

"I writhed in agony at that hospital," I say, my voice shaking. "It was the worst pain I've ever experienced. I did it all for this family. And you…you didn't even have the…the…the dignity to give me so much as a thought. You…"

I've rehearsed this several times but I guess nothing can prepare you. The feeling of overwhelm almost knocks me out of my seat. Richard has stopped pacing and is staring desperately at me.

"Don't, Keren," he whispers.

I shake my head.

"I'm not leaving you," I say. "I don't want that. We've built a life together. We both made vows."

I take a deep breath, wipe my eye and straighten up.

"You need to sort yourself out. Otherwise – goddammit, Richard – I *will* walk away and you will never see Freya again. I brought her into this world, I can take her out of yours. Don't you forget that."

He strides towards me, hoping to pull me into an embrace of sorts. I point my knife in his direction and he halts.

"Off you go."

He scarpers.

Satisfied, but by no means full, I return all my attention to the lasagna. It really is delicious. I'm feeling energised. Some women say consuming the placenta improves milk supply, combats postpartum depression and boosts mood. Right now, it might just be a placebo effect, but who knows?

# PODRIDO

"Miguél is in town, you know."
The coffee cup in my hand shook violently. I placed it on the saucer and looked at my uncle as he took another puff of his pipe, the smoke billowing into the thick summer air. My uncle's face was impassive.

"Is this…because of his father?"

"Yes, Don Vazquez won't be here much longer," my uncle grunted, as if he were talking about the rain rather than our neighbour and friend of many years. I gazed across Plaza del Pueblo, at the narrow strip of sunshine that had found gap a between the houses and was brutally beaming down on the cobblestones. So, there it was. Miguél had finally decided to show his face again after all these years. I found myself reaching for a cigarette.

"Is he alone?" I asked.

"It appears so," my uncle said. "Were you hoping to see Isabel?"

My heart surged at the mention of her name. It had been a long time since I had heard the delicate whispers of those three syllables out loud, even longer since I had heard them escape from my own lips. It was every day, however, that I thought about her, even if just for a second whilst tying my shoelaces, puffing on a cigarette, closing up shop.

"No," I replied, taking another draw.

My uncle grunted. He did not know the full story. I gulped down the rest of my coffee and stood up. "*Hasta luego, tío.*"

My uncle gave me a half-wave. I walked down Calle Emilio Castelar and onto Calle Colón, sucking on the cigarette until the smoke choked me and I threw it onto the ground. The townspeople of Buñol were excited. It was the first time in a long time that we were due to host La Tomatina, and everybody I passed on the street was either inebriated or preparing the exterior of their home for the impending bedlam of crowds pelting each other with tomatoes. Last year a huge tomato had been carried through the streets in a coffin as a sign of protest against the man responsible for banning the festival.

My uncle had said that if he ever met him, he would do worse things to General Franco than pelt tomatoes at him, but at the same time parading a particularly gargantuan piece of fruit through our town was just plain ridiculous, and there were bodies lying in ditches across our country that no-one could identify or retrieve, let alone mourn.

My father, unlike my uncle, had been an exceptional man in more ways than one. At six foot four, with alarmingly thick eyebrows and skin smoother than a ripe tomato, he had put the grandest of sequoia trees to shame, and I looked up to him (literally and figuratively.) He had been a man of stories, devoted to books and the art of writing, but also a businessman, with an undeniable aptitude for honest communication, crunching numbers and anticipating the emergence of competitors. My father's business venture had begun with Papeleria de Meraça, a humble stationer's right at the heart of Buñol, where I was born in 1920. I used to ask him why he had settled on pens and paper rather than books, and his response was always, "a pen and paper together create the foundation upon which great stories unfurl themselves. Also, I'd never get any work done if I owned a bookshop." Papeleria de Meraça had been the start and simultaneously the end of my father's enterprise. It became mine shortly after I turned eighteen. This wasn't a gift from my father to me, not some sort of early inheritance, but an accident. My father completely disappeared, lost in the sea of many others who had vanished without a trace during the civil war. Perhaps I'd have taken over the business eventually had he not disappeared. There is no way to know, no mirror onto which the glimpse of another life can be reflected. That was another thing he used to tell me. As a young man I'd often wake in the night, having dreamt my father was standing, somehow, on the glass surface of a calm sea, and all the world was a muted grey.

I walked, sweating. Learning that Miguél was in town had thrown up many emotions at once. When I looked up into the blinding face of the sun, it was memories that flashed before me, more dizzying than any ultraviolet rays. I went home, slept, then returned to the store for a few hours, though of course the influx of clientele was minimal given that everybody was busy preparing for tomorrow. Señora Fuentes came in to buy a new fountain pen, grumbling ceaselessly about it being impossible to attend mass because of all the festivities. Whilst she prattled on, all I could think about was closing up shop and getting severely drunk. And I did – one minute before six I locked the doors and went in search of beer. I was intoxicated within half an hour, given that I had not eaten a single thing. I did not go to the traditional paella contest as I knew it would be heaving with people and I did not want to bump into Miguél there. I stumbled into bed at four o'clock in the morning and lay awake listening to the dragon-like snoring of my uncle in the other room.

When I did fall asleep, I dreamt of Isabel Vilaró. Though I thought about her daily, I did not often dream of her; the weight of her absence was a load too heavy for my subconscious. Without a shadow of a doubt, Isabel was the only woman I had ever loved. I had not even bothered to look elsewhere since she had left Buñol; I knew pretty much everyone in town, and no other woman could compare to her. Neighbours were like your extended family in Buñol. Perhaps, if I had given out multiple chances to well-meaning girls, I would have found someone I could have borne living with, perhaps someone who I would have grown fond of and for whom I would have thought about buying flowers. But as the pain was too severe, what point was there sticking plasters when my flesh had been lacerated?

Isabel's father owned a vineyard.

It was situated just outside of town; hours outside in the sun meant his skin was a deep olive, and Isabel had inherited his complexion. She loved the outdoors, and used to write poetry about the mountain ranges she could see from the canopies, La Sierra de Las Cabrillas, de Dos Aguas and de Malacara y Martés. She came into my father's shop to buy her pens and paper, and it was not unusual for me to slip her extra ink or paper free of charge. I always wanted to see her poetry, but she would not show me and blushed whenever I asked her about it.

Miguél was also fond of her. Then again, he found beauty and virtue in everyone. He had piercing blue eyes and a wide mouth, which made him seem as if he were always smiling, rendering him likeable from the outset. I enjoyed the fact that everybody liked him when they met him, without him even needing to try, because they ended up liking me, too. I never really thought that eventually, I would come to resent the fact that because he didn't have to try, no-one would suspect him of having the ability to crush a man's soul.

I had loved my father wholeheartedly. I had

loved Isabel, I had loved Miguél, but I had loved my mother in the way a child is obliged to love their mother. It is more of an acceptance, tinged with gratitude when life is good and always resentment when life is not so good. The best way to describe my mother would be a watercolour painting. Her skin was milky, eyes a grey-blue, and there were too many layers to her, undercurrents of emotion that would reveal themselves at different intervals. She had a kind face, but she would often nit-pick or make a fuss over nothing, justifying this by saying she only wanted everything to be perfect. When my father disappeared, she sank into a bottomless pit of despair and anguish; the muted blue of her eyes became constantly saturated by tears. Like a painting, her edges became blurred, and it took four years of nebulous existence before she decided to bite the bullet and take her own life, overdosing on pills she stole from the *farmacia.* Why she didn't pay for the pills will always remain a mystery. Perhaps the exchange of money would have made the whole ordeal too real; by that point the concept of my father was neither real nor hypothetical, and perhaps her own concept of reality had been steadily unravelling.

When I awoke it was early. My head pounded and my mouth tasted like the bottom of a *cuadra del burro*, but I had to rouse myself as I was yet to prepare the shop and my own home for La Tomatina, which was due to commence in a matter of hours.

After I had finished with the preparations, I lit a cigarette, and decided I would lessen the initial pain of seeing Miguél by greeting him on my own terms.

Knocking on the heavy door of the Vazquez household, I realised I had been holding my breath for some seconds. When Miguél appeared in front of me, the strangest feeling settled over my chest. It was as if he were both a stranger and an old friend. He looked leaner now, and the wrinkles etched onto his skin were more defined; the rat-race of Madrid had obviously aged him. Despite this, he had an air of confidence about him. He had also grown a moustache. I didn't know what to say, do, or think.

"Ishmael de Meraça!"

He said this very slowly. For a second, my heart skipped a beat and we were teenagers once again. He may have looked different but underneath the hair of his upper lip I recognised the boyish smile that I could only ever associate with better times. He thumped my shoulder cheerfully and the motion jolted me back to the present.

"You're looking well, Ishmael. It's good to

see you."

"I…" I cleared my throat. "Thank you. *Bienvenido*."

He thumped my shoulder again, softer this time. His piercing eyes were lingering on me, and I was expecting the hurt and rage and disgust to come flooding back. To my vexation, nothing happened. Time seems to function of its own accord and whilst doing so, shows absolutely no mercy. It quickens during the moments you long to keep hold of, stretches out in a way that makes the most excruciating of circumstances seem to last forever. It pits two people against each other, allowing a safe space for one heart to grow fonder and one heart to harden. I was sure my heart had hardened, but all time had done, apparently, was numb it.

*"¿Quién esta ahí?"*

Miguél's father was barely audible; his deep voice had been reduced to a wheeze, and you didn't need to see the man to know that he would soon no longer be here.

"Ishmael de Meraça," called Miguél. I looked for any sign of scorn or ridicule.

I followed Miguél into the room where his father was sitting, small and withered like a raisin. He had no knowledge of what had passed between Miguél and I, as far as I was aware. After Miguél had left town we would bump into one another each week, and he would tell me what a shame it was that fate had cruelly separated us. I would nod and smile and say *así es la vida*, but I wondered if he ever noticed the way my arms would break out into goose pimples at the mere mention of Miguél's name, or the tensing of my jaw.

"How amazing it is to see the two of you together in the same room," said Don Vazquez, flashing a toothless smile. "*Mis dos hijos*. My two sons."

A wave of emotion came out of nowhere, because I remember when Miguél and I were, indeed, like brothers. For a moment or two I felt what could only be described as shock at the lunacy of the universe, the ways in which relationships can shift like tectonic plates and there being nothing you can do but accept it. I was scared of this overwhelming feeling taking hold of me, so I asked Don Vazquez how he was feeling and he said, "better now that you two are standing before me."

There was nothing to do but excuse myself, saying I had errands to run. As I left the house the sunlight threw itself over me and I walked at a madman's pace, marvelling at the fact that I had been waiting for this moment for so, so long.

When my mother died, I went to live with my uncle. My aunt had left for France during the war and had taken the children with her. She had no intention of coming back, and my uncle never spoke about her. We had a good, simple relationship. He was not a businessman but helped me during my initial years running the Papeleria. We tended to limit our conversation to domestic and professional operations, or the latest news from Valencia – or the football. We were two men clinging to one another like fresh pages of a book, the inexorable pain of loss wedged somewhere deep within us, and prising us apart meant exposing an Iliad that would not even come close to classical.

"Please leave all the beer within arm's reach," my uncle grunted. He was staying at home for the whole day and did not plan on leaving the house unless the police were specifically offering people wads of cash in the street. I was drinking a coffee and smoking, for I did not know what else to do with myself. It was almost time for the hoisting of the palo-jabón, and I thought about the fact that people would be scrambling to pull down a piece of ham while my life had unexpectedly come full circle.

I went into the kitchen to fetch the cold beers from the refrigerator. As I opened the door, I did not realise there was a wine glass perched on the side, still half full. Within a second it had fallen to the floor and shards of glass had scattered across the room, leaving a bloody trail. I swore under my breath, knowing it was me who had staggered home the night before and poured myself a drink that I was evidently too drunk to finish. I quickly set about cleaning up the mess before the red wine left a stain I couldn't shift. The stench of the liquid turned my stomach, and I knew the best thing to do would be to go straight to bed, avoiding the crowds and the alcohol and the streets that would soon be coated in red, avoiding Miguél and the confusion that had seized my body when I had seen his face for the first time in so long.

What many people don't know about La Tomatina is that the tomatoes used are not suitable for sale and are inadequate for consumption. Thus, it is not a waste of good quality produce, more a declaration of commitment to the upholding of standards amongst our fine Valencian people. Things that aren't good enough can be turned into sources of entertainment, like whores, or unsavoury politicians. Why waste such things?
*And why waste a moment?* The streets were busier than I'd ever seen them. People had heard about the return of the celebration and

had obviously come from far and wide to be a part of it. Surrounding me were grinning faces, smiles so wide that I felt the inexplicable urge to knock some teeth out. The sun was blisteringly hot already. There would be feverish joy for an hour, then many more hours of exhausting clean-up. Soon the burst tomatoes would be simmering on the stones and the stench of sweat would permeate the plazas. In my shaken state, going outside was an assault on the senses, but I had no choice.

I welcomed being doused in water by the hoses. It refreshed me in such a way that my head became clear enough to aid me in finding Miguél. As the tomatoes plummeted through the air with the force of bullets, I watched one lady be carried away, screaming. There were many more who, jarred by the sea of red and the fistfuls of burst skins and juices, wrestled to escape the crowds, and I suddenly understood the raw pain that was hitting people just as hard as the tomatoes. The frenzy only made me more determined, more charged. I had never been so set upon anything in my entire life. Even this thought made me angrier – with myself – and I clawed at innocent bystanders until they twisted away from me and I pushed myself through.

Another thing people don't know about La

Tomatina is that the citric acid in the tomatoes leads to the streets of Buñol, after being washed, becoming impeccably clean.

Miguél had not seen me. A young girl had made him her target, and Miguél was laughing, making a show of cowering from her. This playfulness reminded me that the man was human whether I liked it or not, and as I stood there, I wished I hadn't directly witnessed such a joyful scene. Simultaneously I resented the fact that he had the capacity for laughter, for enjoying the little things in life, and I didn't. I hadn't for such a long, long time, and it was this thought that drove me towards him.

The crowd surged suddenly and I panicked, thinking I had lost sight of him. It would be easy; within my field of vision were hundreds of flailing hands and slippery figures amid a sea of red. Someone careered to the right and there in full view the pulp meandered down Miguél's broad back. Adrenaline cruised through me, pushing me so hard that I almost stumbled into him, and then I took the knife out. In one quick moment it was done – I couldn't risk a second time – and I heard the noise as Miguél sucked in his breath and turned his head to look at me. I began to push through the crowds, knowing it would only be later that someone would stop to realise it was blood, rather than the juice of the tomatoes, which ran out of a wound in Miguél's side. It should have ended there and then, but as dire chance would have it, there was another crowd surge and I found myself rolling backwards and pressed up against Miguél. I tried unsuccessfully to escape, giving him several seconds to piece together what had just happened and me several seconds to plunge myself into a pit of vehement self-loathing.

It would seem impossible, given that the air was thunderous with shouts and laughter and screaming, but I could hear every raspy exhalation from Miguél's lips. I knew he was fighting internally with himself over what, if anything, to say to me, just as I was. I felt his legs buckling but there was no room for him to fall. He grabbed my arm, nearly pulling it from the socket.

"Ishmael," he said, his voice barely wavering. I wondered if I would faint.

"No," was the only word I could muster, retrieving my arm. But he knew there was nowhere for me to run.

"You fool." Tears began to run down his cheeks.

"You are the fool," I said. "I…you have no idea of the pain you have caused me. I was your *friend*."

Any second and the whole crowd would know what I had done. I wrestled to get away from Miguél, but there were five or six drunken men behind me, swaying like trees, yelling and hollering. The tears began to cascade down my own face, mingled with my sweat and the pulp of those blasted tomatoes.

"Isabel was too good for you," I gasped.

"When Isabel learns of this, she will be devastated," Miguél uttered. "She will be heartbroken. But not as heartbroken as I am."

I had thought about this moment many times. I had used the hatred within me as fuel to carry on. Or so I thought. Perhaps the hatred had dissipated over time, as I had learned after seeing Miguél's face for the first time yesterday. But the seed had been planted for so long, and I had spent years nurturing it, that to give up now would be to admit a defeat like no other.

Though sweat poured from Miguél's brow as he struggled against death, still he found the strength and tenderness to reach up and stroke my cheek. I froze, and he smiled.

*"Why don't you shout?" Ishmael stuttered.*

*"Because they will arrest you. You will make the headline as the first man to commit murder at La Tomatina. But you cannot have the spectacle or the predictable ending. You*

*will have to live with this for the rest of your life. You will be tormented by it. You won't take your own life, because you are too much of a coward."*

*Ishmael gazed at Miguél. Then, as if snapping out of a trance, he batted Miguél's fingers away.*

*"You call me a coward?"*
*Miguél's eyes were soft.*

*"You never had the balls to confront me about anything," he murmured. "You didn't even have the balls to fight me, man to man. You found a way to hide. Even now, you are doing the same thing. The blood coming from this wound you cannot see. But...I am a coward, too."*

*The tears flowed.*

*"I was scared to admit the truth, Ishmael. It was never Isabel. I did everything just to make her happy, thinking it would make me happy, too, thinking I would have a chance at a normal life. It was all in vain. All..." He faltered. "All of it. Everything."*

*Miguél wept. The noise of the fiesta seemed to melt away, leaving behind a deafening silence. The men behind were jostling, impaling, and bruising Ishmael, who welcomed the blows. Before him, a thousand memories rose up like ghosts. He looked past Miguél and saw a man raising his face to the sky, hair slicked black and body crimson all over. For a split second, Ishmael thought the man was the devil. Trembling and crying, Ishmael began to recite.*

*"Dios te salve, María, llena eres de gracia, el Señor es contigo, bendita tú eres entre todas las mujeres…"*

*He was aware that he still had the knife. He raised it a second time.*

# HARD TO SWALLOW

Friday evening; the Central Line. Zoe is wedged between a man that smells like feet and an enormous backpack. She needs to shit, desperately. She closes her eyes, willing her bowels to *fucking keep it together,* but thinking about it makes it worse, like when you need to pee and you imagine swimming in a lake. It disgusts Zoe how much she thinks about excretion. She imagines a desert, but the carriage is sweltering, hence the tangy odour of feet.

She had been fine all day – this is what's most annoying. It was probably the stress of getting on the train, knowing it was going to be absolutely heaving with bodies. Zoe attempts to distract her own body by people-watching, which isn't exactly easy when your line of sight is blocked by multiple limbs. There are no personal boundaries on the Tube, of course. That's until somebody coughs or sneezes and the crowd backs away as much as possible. Sometimes Zoe feels like the IBS defines her, the sweating and stabbing pains guiding her every moment like two proud parents who have raised their girl just right. To Zoe it feels more like a demon living inside of her, cracking its knuckles every so often.

The man with the fuck-off backpack is so tall his head almost touches the ceiling. He's got hair on every visible surface of skin. Zain's pretty hairy, although he keeps it under control. Frequent trips to the barbers. Comes back with his barnet cropped and sleek, head like some sort of sculpture you'd see in a gallery – handsome and symmetrical. Zoe rests her head on her aching arm and cannot wait to get home so he can shower her with sympathy. She spots a girl nearby eating a steak and cheese sub, grease glistening on her lips. Zoe hasn't had a Subway in years. Her stomach grumbles. The girl takes another ravenous bite, like someone who hasn't eaten all day. *That could probably kill me,* Zoe thinks, and listens to the rumble of the train.

She's pulled him into a hug.

"Just feel like crap," Zoe says. "No pun intended."

Zain grins.

"PJ here?" he asks.

"Somewhere." Zoe proceeds to hurtle his name across the flat.

PJ emerges from the kitchen with an assortment of vegan titbits rolling around on a dining plate. He's in a onesie.

"You made it out alive, then," remarks PJ, who would rather die than get on the Tube.

"Just about," says Zoe.

"Good to see you, Mister Rahman. What you saying?"

"I'm good, bro." Zain and PJ thrust their knuckles forward simultaneously. Zoe feels the familiar, warm glow of contentment as her two dearest friends display their affection for one another. The pain is temporarily lifted as she remembers how grateful she is for good things.

"What's on the agenda tonight, then?" Zoe asks PJ.

"Snacks, meditation, dinner, Grindr, *Gray's Anatomy*. In that order."

"Fun!"

"Would have been more fun with my *housemate*, but it's calm, I'll allow you. And your boyfriend."

Zain grins sheepishly.

"Safe, bro."

Zoe, ever baffled by the London lingo, lets out a chuckle.

"I see you *every day*. Didn't realise you were so needy!" she says, and thrusts a jesting fist into PJ's pillowy upper arm.

"Hun, don't flatter yourself, I'm not that desperate for your company." PJ walks off, cackling, and Zoe grins, leading Zain into the kitchen.

"Friday nights are usually us slobbing about in front of the TV," Zoe explains to Zain whilst pouring herself a glass of water.

"Well, I'm not sorry for stealing you tonight," Zain replies, winding his arms around Zoe's waist as she stands by the sink. He kisses her neck. Zoe is collared by that delicious feeling in her groin, then feels a single stabbing pain in her gut. As expected. She turns around, glass in hand, and kisses Zain's mouth.

"Don't know how much fun I'll be."

"You might feel better after you've eaten." A cruel paradox if ever there was one.

Zoe turns the oven on, then starts chopping up asparagus. Zain takes charge of the potatoes. Their dinner tonight will also include salmon; Zoe might add some garlic butter if she's feeling adventurous.

"How's PJ doing?" Zain asks.

"Yeah, he's good. He had some stuff going on with his mum recently but it's all okay now. I think he's thriving, to be honest."

"Yeah?"

"Yeah, totally. He loves his job, loves the flat, he's got such a solid group of friends. A tribe, you know?"

"Mmm."

"They're all about body positivity and crystal healing and activism and whatnot. It's funny though…I mean, not funny, but…you know, for *me*, he's such a close friend and obviously I don't know a huge amount of people in London, but I think for him – because he's got *so* many friends – I'm just one out of, like, a hundred. D'you know what I mean?"

"Yeah…I get you. But you're still close, innit? He might be the more sociable one out of the two of you but it doesn't mean that he sacrifices the quality of his other strong relationships, like the one you guys have."

"True. I think he's just like a magnet…people want to be around him, and he wants to get to know as many people as possible. He's got quite a big family as well, so it makes sense, whereas I'm the opposite. Small family, small group of friends. I mean…I suppose I'm happy with that."

Zoe flashes a smile.

"Yeah, maybe," says Zain. "Or maybe you were desperate for some spice in your life to shake things up and that's why you pounced on me."

Zoe chucks the tea towel at him.

"Whatever you might think, you're not my token person of colour," Zoe says wryly. "PJ's already fulfilled the role."

"Ha!"

Zain tosses the potatoes into a large pan.

"Speaking of brown people, how you feeling about tomorrow?"

The tightening in Zoe's chest and the second sharp, stabbing pain in her gut speak for themselves, but Zoe forces a smile.

"Fine, why?"

"Just asking."

"Yeah." Zoe shrugs, feigning nonchalance. "Who's going again?"

"My sisters, a couple of Hamida's friends, maybe a couple cousins. My parents ain't."

Zoe nods, wondering if she will ever actually get to meet Zain's parents. She can't decide whether she'd rather prolong the tension or get it over with. Maybe there isn't much point – unless she decides to marry. After only nine months of dating Zain this isn't exactly on the horizon. Zoe reconsiders her very recent epiphany regarding contentment. Is she content? *Decided to move to the most expensive place in the country to work, fell in love with a Muslim, constantly clashing with large intestine…are things rosy?* Zoe is aware that this is a dumb spiral of self-destruction that she need not fall into – her body is perfectly capable of self-destruction without any assistance. *Positives, Zoe, positives.* London is fantastic, and Zain wouldn't be sticking around if this relationship wasn't worth it, right? As for the large intestine…Zoe yawns. The Drowsy Stage. This is how it goes every time. Shit, pain, sleep, not necessarily in that order. Zoe makes a mental note to scan the restaurant menu at the earliest opportunity. She wonders if Zain's uncle will like her.

"Zoe."

Zoe looks up.

"Go and relax."

Zoe hesitates, then smiles and graciously departs.

The next day, she is in the kitchen making poached eggs. It's midday but she's in her dressing gown, auburn hair springing from a hastily assembled bun. PJ saunters in, slightly taken aback, as he always is, by his housemate's paper-white face, devoid of make-up, dotted with light freckles. He's always stunned by the unnerving absence of melanin. But he also likes how Zoe looks –

it's striking. Ginger people generally are. She definitely needs some eye gel to combat those bags, though.

"I want some advice," PJ says, opening the fridge.

"Is it worth asking me," says Zoe, "when you do your own thing anyway?"

PJ grins, unscrewing the lid of his carton of coconut water.

"You're right, I think I'll just talk, and you can add comments if you want." Zoe nods, watching the eggs but listening intently. "I'm going to my Mum's, yeah? So, do I eat beforehand so that I'm full and have an excuse to not eat curry goat, or do I take my own food with me so I don't get hungry because nothing will be vegan? Nah, that's rude...*or* do I just go and be like, 'I'm taking this seriously, I'll just eat the rice and some salad.' I could pretend I'm on a diet. Fuck's sake...every option results in my Mum cussing me anyway."

Zoe lets out a snort.

"It's not funny, I'm lowkey stressing out," says PJ, though the right side of his mouth has been hoisted up into a half grin.

"Just go and be honest," Zoe says, knowing that PJ is about to take the piss out of her.

"*Just go and be honest,*" PJ echoes, as

expected. His forehead is creased and his eyes are narrowed. "I'm not you, you know."

"You've got no problems being honest, PJ," Zoe says, not wanting to unpack his last comment. The eggs are nearly ready, so she pops two slices of bread into the toaster.

"It's just one day, innit?" PJ takes a large swig of coconut water. "Just one day…and the rest of my life."

Zoe thinks about meeting Zain's family.

"I don't know, PJ, all I can say is that…you know, you've got a choice. I get stressed because if I ate fucking…garlic bread, I wouldn't be able to function."

Zoe knows she probably shouldn't have said this, but the thought of the dinner later is niggling at the back of her head like a blister.

"Don't get me started, Chapman."

Out comes PJ's admonishing tone. Zoe doesn't *want* to get him started, but it's too late.

"You *know* how I feel about this whole idea of preference. It ain't a preference; *I* see it as a duty and that's how I think the rest of the world should see it. I'm not doing it because it's fucking fun. It's called sacrifice–"

"Okay, okay, yeah."

"I've got the means to do it, so why wouldn't I do it, you get me?"

"I do. Get you. I'm sorry. You don't need

to tell *me* this. This is what you should be saying to your family."

"Oh, they're gonna get it."

Fired up, PJ tosses the carton into the bin. He stalks towards the door but pauses by the handle.

"If I don't see you, good luck tonight," he says.

Zoe's heart lurches. She flashes PJ a soft smile.

"Yeah, you too."

Zoe knows there is a mutual discomfort they share; maybe it's not about who has it worse, really. She assembles the eggs on toast.

The door opens, and PJ's Mum Denise, with her shiny face devoid of fine lines, stretches her arms wide, encasing him in a hug that reminds PJ of being a kid, and he can feel her bangles jangling and smell the Cantu cream.

"Son, how you been? Keeping well, yeah?"

"Yeah, yeah, yeah, Mum, I'm good, I'm good."

"*Aright*, that's what I like to hear, that's good, P."

PJ enters the house and it smells so good that he feels his eyes watering. He can hear faint music and laughter, wonders who has shown up as his Mum never mentioned names, only told him that she wanted to host a little gathering to celebrate the cancer in her left breast finally relinquishing its efforts to tear her torso apart. *No wonder she's glowing,* PJ thinks, and makes his way to the living-room after hanging up his jacket.

The whole gang is here: Denise's brother, Uncle Clive; sister, Auntie Jackie; the latter's three kids, Rianne, Michael and Daniel; Rianne's four-year-old, Jada, and PJ's sister, Leah. Nan sits in the armchair, half-asleep, but her milky eyes enlarge as PJ's voice booms across the room.

"He's back and better than ever!"
Hugs from the adults, a clumsy embrace from Jada and friendly beats from his sister, who still lives at home with Mum. PJ stoops down to plant a kiss on Nan's cheek, and she grumbles something about seeing him as often as she sees the DPD courier, because he can never find her yard, which makes PJ feel bad but everybody else laugh.

PJ eases himself back into the family as if stepping into a hot bath. Denise is in the kitchen with Leah and Rianne, food prepping though mostly yelping with laughter. There is a glass of Scotch nearby. PJ plays wist and rummy with Auntie Jackie and the boys; Auntie Jackie demolishes them all. Fat Uncle Clive sits by Nanny because he expends so much energy just moving and talking. Eventually the food is ready, and they traipse into the kitchen, animated, PJ leading Nan through in an attempt to win her affections back (though he knows it's futile.) Once she sees his plate, she'll be giving him the third degree.

Incidentally, this doesn't happen; Nan just sits there eyeing him up with a disgruntled look. Perhaps nothing else can disappoint her. She's probably realised he doesn't like girls and all.

"So, what you gonna eat, then?" asks Rianne sassily, hand on hip, other hand still clutching the serving spoon that is submerged in curry goat slop.

"Rice and plantain, innit," says PJ, as if it's a silly question. If he plays it cool and doesn't make it sound like a big deal, then maybe everybody else will feel dumb for making it seem like one. "And salad."

"What's he saying, Ri?" Denise is taking the macaroni pie out the oven, and Jada has just screeched in delight. "You not eating meat again, PJ?"

"I told you already, Mum…"

Denise kisses her teeth and gestures to the multiple dishes spread out across the kitchen counters.

"Afta mi just spent all dis time slaving away…PJ! What's going on? You sick?" She approaches her son with the oven gloves, pressing her hand against his forehead. Laughter.

"Mum, come on, I've been vegan for like, three months now."

"What did he say, Den?" calls Auntie Jackie. The music's too loud and PJ can feel himself getting hot.

"He says he's a *veeegan*," Denise calls, and the word, stretched out like a stick of chewing gum, pings across the room. Auntie Jackie shakes her head and chuckles. The boys are laughing, though a tiny part of PJ thought they'd have his back, considering it's not so weird these days.

"So he doesn't eat meat?"

"What about the macaroni?"

"Nah, Mum, he can't eat that either," Leah pipes up, already halfway through a leg of chicken. Auntie Jackie is leaning across the table and asking the boys if *they* knew PJ was allergic to animals.

"Guys, it's not that deep, let me just enjoy my rice and plantain. And salad," says PJ, flustered, fumbling for cutlery.

"The macaroni hasn't got meat in it," Denise repeats, equally as flustered. Jada is pulling at the hem of her jeans; she picks her up and coos: "You want some, bubba?"

"It's dairy, Mum, no cheese, no milk.

Rianne, can you make me a drink?"

"Prentice James, are you having me on?" Denise says, dropping Jada to the floor again with a bit too much force.

"It's not personal," PJ says, finding a vacant chair.

"He thinks it's cruel, Mum," says Leah, picking at the bone. "Eating animals."

"Yeah, but it's not just that…"

PJ swore he wouldn't get into politics whilst at the dinner table. He feels weird; he's had conversations at house parties about veganism, at work, in the cloakroom queue with strangers on a Saturday night. But here, in the comfort of his own home…well, it just doesn't feel right. In fact, he'd rather not mention it at all.

Too late now.

"So no cheese? No chicken? No pork? No…" Michael is racking his brains for more prohibited foodstuffs.

"Chocolate!" Daniel adds. There are loud groans, as if PJ's personal decision is causing the rest of them indescribable pain.

"Eggs!" yelps Auntie Jackie. "There are eggs in a lot of things. How does that work, then?"

"Is it for your health, PJ?" Rianne asks, handing him a drink. PJ starts gulping it down.

"Health? He'll kill himself!" Auntie Jackie squawks.

Uncle Clive, sat to the left of PJ, has done nothing but eat and chortle. This time around he chokes and falls victim to a bout of coughing; PJ thumps his back, wishing they could move on.

"That's it, PJ, that's what worries me," says Denise, still standing. She doesn't seem to be able to sit down and relax until the matter is resolved. "You know…it's about protein, isn't it? It's about getting the right nutrients. It can't be healthy."

PJ slams his fork down.

"First of all," he says, "there are *bare* things you can eat to get protein. Lentils. Chickpeas. Beans. Tofu. Oats. Nuts. Seeds. I'm sick of people asking me where I get my protein from. Secondly, think of all that shit that the goats and the cows and the pigs and the chickens eat, shoved together in barns, rolling around in their own shit, pumped with hormones. Thirdly, it's been proven – *proven* – that there's a strong association between red meat and carcinogens, as in cancer, as in disease, as in *death*."

He stabs at a slice of cucumber. When he glances upwards, Mum's face hardens and then softens, the eyebrows drifting upwards, mouth tightening. PJ is perturbed for a second, then realises what he's said. The whole table is suddenly quiet except for Jada, who pops a morsel of chicken into her mouth and chews as if her teeth are chattering. Ordinarily PJ would look gravely upon the scene, thinking about how kids are conditioned to get excited about animals whilst at the same time being forced to consume them, but right now he can only look at his Mum – until he can't. He lowers his gaze and takes a gulp of Scotch.

"Imagine just eating nuts all the time," says Michael tactfully. The ice is broken, and there are titters.

"If you ask me, being vegan is for the *white* people dem," Leah adds, somewhat scornfully. Murmurs of agreement. PJ rolls his eyes; he's mentioned Rastafarians and Hindus more times than he can count.

"All of us sitting here can afford to eat less meat," he says. "I'll bet you any money I spend less on my shopping than you lot do." Denise kisses her teeth.

"Alright, alright, we get it," she says. "It's not a competition. PJ does what makes PJ happy, innit. Cheers to independence."

She raises a glass and the rest of the family happily oblige, including PJ. He looks at his Mum and attempts a smile; she gives him a look that can only mean *you're lucky you don't live here now.*

Zoe and Zain walk out of Aldgate East station and towards Brick Lane. It's at times like this that Zoe gets an overwhelming sense of how exciting London is. Her chest tightens as they approach New Spice, Uncle Abdul's infamous curry house that is, at present, jam-packed. Waiters dart between tables, photographs of the staff and B-list celebrities adorn the walls. Zain pushes open the door and they are greeted by the hubbub. A large man with a fresh haircut and small eyes sallies up to them, beaming.

"Long time!" he says, pulling Zain into an embrace.

"*Sasa,* this is Zoe."

Uncle Abdul tilts his head courteously.

"Welcome, welcome. I hope you like it here. Please, come."

He leads them through the restaurant and downstairs, where a long table and Hafsa's party are waiting. Zoe is expecting a band of Zain's relatives, ready to scrutinize her and her ginger hair. Instead, she is relieved to find a group of twenty somethings, talking and giggling innocuously, most of them engrossed in mobile phones. Zain greets the entourage and is met with a chirpy response; his sisters stand up in succession and are excited to see

Zoe. They hug. Hafsa, Hamida and Zuhi are slender and smell like perfume. Hamida looks stunning as per usual; her make-up is blended to perfection and she's wearing a brown hijab elegantly assembled into something of a turban.

"Congratulations, Hamida," Zoe says, handing her the gift bag.

"Aww, thanks, Zoe!" she squeals, pulling Zoe into another hug. "You honestly shouldn't have. It was just a driving test."

"How many minors did you get this time?" asked Zain. "Seven?"
Hamida swats him playfully.

"At least I've *passed*, unlike some people…"
Zoe sits next to Zain, with Zuhi on her left, the youngest Rahman sister. At just fifteen she's shy and unsure of herself, albeit sweet; Zoe is rather relieved to be in this position as it means she won't have to talk about herself too much. She is torn between wanting to appear cool and confident and wanting to appear laid-back and easygoing. She thinks this will be the right spot at the table, and happily orders a mango lassi.

Hamida is excitable and forgets to introduce Zoe to everyone, so Zain fills her in. Two of Hamida's friends are present, as well as two of Zain's youngest uncles ("they're really chill and only a few years older than me so it's calm.") Aqsa and Nawaf, brother and sister, are cousins ("all our other cousins are ten or younger, so this is the gang as it stands.") Zoe tries to pay close attention but can already feel the names merging into one.

As they scour the menus, the waiter brings out papadums. Zoe piles them onto her plate, relishing the chance at eating something plain. She chats to Hafsa and Hamida for a bit, but the menu reels her back in every few minutes. She pores through it. It's huge – there's bound to be something she can eat, surely? Out of the blue, an uncle addresses Zoe from across the table.

"So you're Zain's girlfriend?"

"Guilty," says Zoe.

"Zain, you're punching, man."

Everyone laughs and Zoe laughs with them, blushing.

"Where are you from, Zoe?" asks Aqsa; the conversation has attracted listeners.

"Sheffield originally. Moved here about…two years ago? Something like that."

"Oh, okay."

Uncle Abdul appears with some starters on the house and the conversation grinds to a halt. Zoe turns immediately to Zain.

"What can I have?" she whispers furiously.

"What? Oh. Ermm…shit, I'm not gonna

lie, I think literally everything's got onion or garlic in it, you know. Lemme ask my Uncle just to make you something proper simple, yeah? Like a korma or something but without...er, the onion."

Zoe's face heats up at the thought of Zain asking Uncle Abdul to strip back the already tame korma, leaving it practically naked. She gets up quickly as Uncle Abdul begins to take orders.

"I'll leave it to you. I'm going to the toilet," Zoe hisses.

She sits in the cubicle, breathing heavily. The demon has reared its ugly head and is admonishing Zoe for thinking she could have ever had a good time without it. She stands up but the cramps seem to have taken control over neighbouring territories; her thighs, bum and even back are out of action. Zoe thinks of Zain and his family at the table, laughing and joking, the dishes of food vivid and colourful and aromatic, a snapshot of a vibrant culture. Why did English food have to be so *dull* in comparison? *We must all seem so dull,* Zoe thinks, *so dull that we resorted to stealing bits of culture from practically every other country in the world.* Damn, where did *that* thought come from? Zoe writhes at the idea of her korma arriving – a bland dish for a bland girl. Did Zain's family think she was bland? Bland in comparison to Zain, who is feisty and funny and sweet and who works out and loves kids and has travelled and is somebody that everybody loves. Zoe is twenty-six and Sheffield is just some city up north. Why did she move to London, really and truly? Was it for excitement? All of Zoe's paycheck goes on the rent, and now she's crying in a toilet because PJ will probably move out and she can't eat a fucking onion. If Zain were here, he'd say something like, "well, I didn't think onions were meant to make you cry like *this*." Through her tears, Zoe suddenly laughs.

She forces herself up, blows her nose, wipes her eyes and stumbles back to the table, where fate awaits. When it arrives her bowl of curry sits, shamefully, between Zain's vindaloo and Zuhi's lamb rezala. Zoe eats it without a word, heat rising in her face. The others pile food onto their plates and sweep it up as if it's second nature, while Zoe's stomach and bowels pulsate, ready for their favourite game in which she is the permanent loser. Deal or No Deal. Ingest or Reject.

The others are tactful and say nothing, but Zoe needs to make an exit as soon as humanly possible.

"Zain, I've gotta go," she says, placing her knife and fork down. They are heavy between her fingers, like lead.

Zain's mouth is full of food, but his eyebrows are creased with concern. Zoe shoves a tenner into his pocket, pretends she's had an urgent phone call and dashes up the stairs and out of the restaurant before her boyfriend can protest.

That's when the tears start again.

At ten o'clock Zoe wakes up with a start, having dozed off for an hour or so. The traces of pain from earlier in the evening are gently dissolving, and she's in dire need of a glass of water. The disorientation that only comes from napping is acute, and she gingerly rises from her bed. Yawning, she bumbles towards the kitchen, and is surprised to see PJ sitting under the harsh, fluorescent lights with a plate of food. She's even more surprised to see that he's eating…chicken?

"Hey," she mumbles.

"Hey," he says.

They stare at each other. PJ flings the piece of meat onto the plate and leans back, folding his arms. Then he rubs his face wearily with his hands, hands which Zoe has always found sinewy and rather beautiful.

"I don't even know what to tell you," PJ murmurs.

Zoe looks at the plate of chicken. She considers this for a moment, then searches for a glass.

"What happened?" she asks, running the tap until it gets cold.

PJ sighs.

"It was awkward," he says. "I said my piece, though. Stuck to my guns. But my Mum made me bring back leftovers. Tried to say that I could give them to you. But I knew you wouldn't eat them. So, then I thought, well, it's only gonna go to waste. And that's not what I want. So now I'm here. And it feels fucking weird. But it also tastes so fucking good." He shoots Zoe a pained look. Zoe grins and joins him at the table with the cup of ice-cold water, the safest and gentlest of all consumables. Nothing could be better. But despite this pure, pure substance, this life-giving elixir, Zoe thinks about the fact that there still exists liters and liters of contaminated water unsuitable to drink, and people are drinking it. Somewhere. Zoe's grin fades, and she looks at the chicken on PJ's plate. Considering the wings are fragments of a larger, feather-clad, breathing animal, on the plate they seem distinctly different from their source, pieces of food entirely unrelated to what they had been before. It's all transmutable, nothing is really pure, and no-one is pure, either. There are layers upon layers of history and culture and emotion, like the skin of onions Zoe can't eat, and now PJ is shaking his head and giving in to the choice he has made and also not made, the quiet, unassuming reality of foodstuff as not just foodstuff. As food. And stuff, a lot of stuff.

# BEING HIT BY A SAMOSA ON THE BACK OF THE HEAD

As I was walking down the street, someone lobbed a samosa at my head.

Okay, okay. I don't know if somebody *threw* it at my head. It might have fallen out of a window. It might have been perched on the edge of a windowsill, and somebody might have knocked it by accident. I'm not sure why you would place a samosa so dangerously close to the edge of a windowsill, but that is one possibility. Somebody might have thrown it out of the window *in anger* and it might have accidentally fallen onto my head. If I were angry, a samosa would not be the first thing I'd grab, but perhaps the person was holding said samosa before somebody else cheesed them off. Maybe a little kid launched the samosa out the window. Whatever the case, the samosa landed on my head, and it simultaneously hurt, shocked and angered me.

It's bad enough having *anything* fall on your head (although, admittedly, some things are worse than others.) I think it might just be one of the most shocking things to happen to anyone, because it's just so *unexpected*. There you are, walking along the street, minding your own business, perhaps listening to music or trying to remember if you've got any dog food left or thinking about what to say to your so-called friend the next time you see them and suddenly, BAM. An oblong-shaped parcel slams into your skull. It's not like you can make a quick recovery. You can't just give your head a little pat and carry on walking, showing passers-by that it might as well have been a piece of fluff gently caressing your scalp. It hurts like a *bitch*. I knew the samosa had travelled quite a distance because it felt as if I'd been hit by a rock. You can imagine my surprise when I looked down, swearing profusely, and saw what I'd normally order as a starter at my local Indian lying pathetically on the ground, having just crashed into the back of my head. Because of its triangular shape it may as well have dented my skull.

It's shocking to be hit by something on the head because it hurts, but it also feels – in some strange way – deeply, acutely, profoundly *personal*. It feels like a personal attack, it really does. It temporarily robs you of your dignity, leaving you vulnerable, naked, ashamed. It's a horrible feeling, accident or no accident.

When I looked down at the samosa, lying pathetically on the ground, I was surprised as well as shocked. I know that sounds weird, because shocked and surprised are almost identical emotions, but in this case, yes, I was both surprised and shocked. My ears were ringing and the tears had appeared on cue, but I was trying to suppress them because I didn't want to feel even more embarrassed than I already did. Instead, I focused my attention on the fact that a whole samosa had now gone to waste, at the expense of quite a few of my brain cells. Curiously, the samosa hadn't split open. Maybe it had been stale (and maybe that was the reason somebody had – literally – chucked it away.) But maybe it hadn't been stale, and that made me feel slightly sad and disappointed. Only for a second, because then I went back to being severely cheesed off. In that second, though, I wondered who on earth would have wanted to waste a perfectly good samosa. It's not as if they had tried it and realised it had tasted awful, and *then* decided to lob it, because the samosa, as mentioned, was perfectly intact. It had most definitely been a waste of a Good Samosa. After taking another few seconds to feel disgruntled, I thought about the fact that the samosa, being a perfectly good samosa, had been taken and used as a weapon. Due to the context of the situation, the samosa had gone from being a harmless, inanimate object to something with the potential to cause serious damage. Ultimately, I was okay (if not pretty embarrassed, hurt and cheesed off) however, someone else might not have been so lucky. If one of the three corners had landed in an unsuspecting eye, it might have been a very different scenario. Fortunately for me, I knew I would be able to carry on with my day. If anything, it would make me more cautious, and I would no doubt pay more attention to my surroundings. I probably shouldn't have been thinking about whether or not I had enough dog food – I should have been more organised and checked before I left the house. I also probably shouldn't have been ruminating so hard about my so-called friend and what I was going to say to them the next time I saw them.

All these thoughts had sprung up within about eight seconds. It was only after about eight seconds that I then made an effort to look around and see if anyone had noticed that I had been assaulted. This was another surprising thing. Normally the first thing you do if something embarrassing happens to you in public is to look around wildly, cheeks flaming. I was more concerned with the object that had plummeted into my world *because* it was just so unusual. To my relief, the streets around me were empty and quiet. My heartbeat began to reorient itself. I adjusted my coat, looked around again, looked down at the samosa, and began walking away. A very ordinary thing to do, and yet I was a changed person. Not changed in any significant way but changed all the same. Prior to that moment, I wouldn't have ever believed that of all things, a samosa could shock and disorient me, and yet it had happened. If that were possible, what else?

I had walked about ten yards when I stopped and turned around. There were still no people about, and I just couldn't stop thinking about the fact that the samosa was lying pathetically on the ground. I couldn't tell you why, but I started walking very quickly back to the spot where I had been assaulted. The samosa was still there, as silent as the grave. Before I knew what I was doing, I had retrieved a tissue from my coat pocket and was picking up the samosa. Feeling its weight for the second time sent a jolt through me. I looked around, hoping that some passer-by hadn't chosen this precise moment to appear and had seen me pick up something edible from the dirty floor, but luckily the streets remained calm and quiet. As I resumed my journey, the samosa lying in the palm of my hand, I started to feel slightly creeped out. As you know, I had come face-to-face with many emotions over the past couple of minutes, but fear hadn't really been one of them. If the neighbourhood was so quiet, and there wasn't much going on, where had the samosa actually come from? It was quite a cold day, so I didn't think many people would have actually had their windows open. It seemed quite a coincidence that I happened to be walking at exactly the right time for the samosa to land exactly on the back of my head, and not my shoulder or ear or something like that. It hadn't grazed the fabric of my coat or fallen into my path; it had hit me right at my weakest spot. Was it some sort of sign? Perhaps that's why I had retraced my steps and picked up the samosa – because subconsciously to leave it would be to ignore the sign. What the sign was I didn't know, but I'm telling you, this little greasy parcel seemed *significant*.

As I walked, the uneasy feeling continued to grow. The streets were deathly quiet. Ten minutes passed and I hadn't seen a single soul. It was an insane sort of exchange – a samosa had dropped out of thin air, and the human race had ceased to exist. I wondered whether there were people out there who had made seriously questionable trade-offs, like Eve jeopardising the whole of humanity for a single, juicy apple. There was probably a schmuck or two who had given up most of their income for some shirt signed by a famous sportsperson, or a man somewhere in the middle east who had traded his daughter for five camels. It is crazy to think of the weight of responsibility people carry, and the fact that often they don't know just quite how heavy this weight is. Humans really, *really* shouldn't be trusted. Imagine being so irresponsible that you think five camels will enhance your life better than your daughter ever could, or you do wild things like throwing samosas out of windows.

The samosa had opened the door to a labyrinth in my mind, in which thoughts were walls and there was seemingly no way out. Because of this, you can imagine the shock and terror that seized me when I accidentally crashed into someone walking the opposite way. The samosa fell from my hand and landed on the ground, and the person I had crashed into swore. I was aghast. Not only had something landed on my head, but now the second worst thing that could possibly happen to someone whilst walking down the street had happened. Bumping into a stranger is awful, because the weight of them is enough for you to clamp your jaws together and do some serious damage to your teeth. The shame and anger I had suppressed earlier came flooding back in tidal waves, and I wanted to cry. I think this came as a shock to the person, because they gave me a look that said 'Jesus Christ, of all the people I could have bumped into!' I attempted to compose myself as the blood rushed to my face, and luckily the person scarpered before anything else could happen. I can't even remember if they apologised or not – I was too busy fending off a shroud of misery. It was like a dark cloud had settled over my head and was raining very heavily on just me. I looked down and the samosa, infuriatingly, was still intact. I was wounded for a second time, and this cunning package hadn't received so much as a scratch. Suddenly, I thought about the fact that I had no idea what was inside the samosa. Was it really packed full of spiced vegetables or mincemeat? Or was there something sinister inside? Was the samosa actually a decoy? My heart began pounding wildly. I ran off before I could find out.

Herein lies my problem. I don't know if you remember but earlier I said that my life had changed. Not in any significant way, but it has changed all the same. I was not the same person I was before I was hit on the head by that samosa. And no matter how hard I try, I cannot go back to a time in which the samosa didn't exist, or the idea of the samosa didn't exist. I have seen the samosa, felt the samosa, and I can never go back to a reality in which I was not affected by that samosa. So now I walk the streets terrified, because even though the samosa is gone, it may still be there. The samosa might be broken, or it might be floating along the canal, or someone might have even digested it, but maybe not. Maybe it is still lying on the ground, winking at anyone who walks past. I should have kept hold of it, or eaten it myself, because then I could at least control the outcome. But the samosa controls me.

My so-called friend has stopped calling. My dog has stopped trying to make me take him out for a walk, because I will not leave the house for fear of what might happen. I am too scared of the possibilities of this life, am terrified at the fact that not everything is what it seems.

This goes for myself, too. And that is the person I am most afraid of. I am afraid of samosas, I am afraid of people, but I am most terrified of myself, because how have I allowed myself to reach this point? How do I escape?

Today I got a leaflet through my door about a new Indian takeaway that is opening down the road. If the samosa wasn't a sign, then this definitely is.

## A BOWLFUL OF MY LOVE

As he hung up the red cloth-banner, Toshiro felt dual spasms of pain in his triceps, the unwelcome reminder that every day he was growing increasingly feeble. Beneath the inky sky, the twin peaches that jutted from the leathery, brown skin of his upper arms looked equal parts impressive and unnerving, Toshiro decided. The air was humid; he felt his back already dripping with sweat, felt the familiar, feverish anticipation of tonight's labour seep through his upper body, a feeling that both roused and fatigued him. Harue had stopped demanding he give it up.
Sometimes Toshiro wanted to, but he almost felt as if he had no choice – it was his vocation, it was, in a sense, part of him. He tended to the *yatai* as if it were just another precious organ,

one that demanded consistent operation in order for Toshiro to function as a human being. Ironically, Harue called him a robot many times for the very same reason.

These were the thoughts that occupied Toshiro's mind as he set up the *yatai*, his pride and joy, one of the last remaining portable food stalls in Bunkyo City – in the whole of Tokyo, as a matter of fact. It was seven in the evening, a Tuesday. Salarymen were still milling about by Suidobashi station, identical in their damp, white shirts, briefcases swinging. Toshiro, as ever, thought about the years under his belt as one of them – a cog in the wheel of a foreign investment bank – the grey hue of life in the office, the innumerable cups of coffee that had stained his teeth and which had steered him away from all forms of caffeine as a retiree. Except he wasn't retired – from the office, yes, but from the stove, never. He had discovered his love for cooking after Harue's accident; she had fallen from a ladder whilst inspecting the kiwi tree, and in those few weeks following – whilst she was in hospital – Toshiro had learnt more about himself than he had during thirty years at the bank. How satisfying and prolific it was to bring together such arbitrary ingredients and fuse them to create flavours that had the power – he was convinced – to release serotonin. Harue had always been a naturally talented cook

and Toshiro had been eating well throughout their marriage but finding the talent within himself had made him proud. Proud and sad, for he had also realised how much time had been wasted. The years seemed to drift away like steam, less and less easy to make out.
Toshiro boiled the water for the ramen.

It was unusually quiet for some time. He did not usually attract hordes of hungry punters, but always enough to fill the evening with quiet chatter, surreptitious murmuring with suit-clad businessmen about controversial political decisions, the incessant clang of the pan lids as Toshiro removed and replaced them. One woman approached him to ask for directions, but she hurried off as quickly as she had arrived. When Toshiro saw the couple making a beeline for the stall – a tall, well-built man and a petite, cherry-lipped young woman, hesitant in their gait but undeniably keen for the warming comfort of noodle soup – his heart did an unexpected somersault. He smiled and welcomed them as one would at a restaurant, because he realised that the routine of each evening had rendered him somewhat mechanical in his exchanges (perhaps Harue had been on to something) and also the man, whose face was warmly familiar, like a song one remembers from childhood or a cup of tea, seemed to light up at the sight of Toshiro, which

Toshiro branded as an unusual occurrence because it was normally the food that brought out the smiles. The two of them sat down – the woman first, pushing her hair behind her ears (an action that she would undertake consistently over the course of the next hour, Toshiro soon discovered.) Toshiro was immediately intrigued by the arrival of these customers. They were Japanese – there was no doubt about that – but they seemed paradoxically at home and adventitious, like people stumbling out of a dark house into the harsh light of day after spending too much time together. They were most likely in love, in that semi-permanent state of wild oblivion. Love did that to people – made them feel both comfortable and keyed up at the same time. Toshiro couldn't resist a smile as he watched the man settle down beside his companion. He then turned his attention to polishing the bowls.

"You've become something of a local legend," the man said, leaning forward slightly. His voice was raised; perhaps he thought Toshiro was hard of hearing.

Toshiro was not shocked that his *yatai* was at the heart of distant conversations, but he found himself pleasantly surprised that this man, in whom he had taken a particular interest, seemed to be just as interested in Toshiro.

"The hard work paid off," he said. "What can

I get you?"

"What would you recommend?"

Toshiro's menu was far from extensive. He saved the complexities of cooking for Harue and himself; his customers were given the choice of two options he had taken time to carefully perfect.

"The standard bowl," he said.

"Not the one with roast pork?"

"Well, it's more expensive."

The man laughed, as did his companion, genuine, unadulterated laughter.

"Have the *chashu*. You can have it for the standard price, no problem," Toshiro said, dropping the noodles into the boiling water.

"Thank you, it does look delicious," said the woman. Every few seconds, Toshiro stole a glance at her, though he was finding it difficult to maintain an air of indifference. The woman was pale, her skin creamy, wearing a dress that was dotted with tiny flowers, the sheen of sweat slick over her clavicle. *Harue would like that dress*, Toshiro thought. He divided soya sauce between the two polished bowls and pretended not to listen to their conversation.

"As the wedding is weeks away," the man was saying, "I think we should get everything out on the table."

Toshiro stole another glance at the woman, realising he had not stumbled upon the passionate unfolding of first love, but what seemed like a potential pre-marital spat. The woman, however, surprised him by chuckling.

"How many secrets are you harbouring?" she asked playfully.

"Well, they aren't secrets, per se, but there must be things we don't know about one another."

Toshiro felt the urge to interrupt but continued to feign ignorance.

"You're right," the woman said, with an acquiescing grin. "Would you like to start, given that it was your idea and there's something you're obviously dying to tell me?"

The man smiled almost mischievously.

"This is how we should do it," he said. "For each ingredient in the ramen, we should disclose one fact."

"You really think I'm withholding that much information?"

"You make it sound almost sinister, my love. Come on, I don't know what you'd do with…with…I don't know, a million dollars."

She looked at him, considering his query. Then she glanced at Toshiro, at their food, and finally returned to gaze at her fiancé.

"Soya sauce – the fate of a million dollars in my hands," she said, and Toshiro instantly knew that their relationship had a poetic quality to it, a youthful energy that made him wistful. The man waited for her answer, expectant, his eyes glittering.

"I guess," she said finally, "I'd give some of the money to charity. I'd invest a chunk. I'd save another chunk for our future. And then…I'd buy a studio. And I'd paint. Eventually I'd open it up for people to use, people that don't have the space or the money or the means to pursue art. People that need an escape."

As the words dropped from her lips, Toshiro poured the soup through a sieve into the bowls. For the first time in a long time, he hoped that the couple would stick around and speak like this late into the night, that the other hungry city-dwellers would find their dinner elsewhere. He pictured a canvas streaked with reds and oranges and purples, dexterous fingers working their magic, and almost lost his breath.

"You don't need a million dollars for that," the man said. "Well, not for the studio. That's what intrigues me the most about your answer. You said all the right things. But your face lit up when you mentioned the studio. Deep down, that's what you want, isn't it?"

"The money is not my money, though. If I were given a million dollars, that money would not belong to me, and so I shouldn't use it solely for myself."

"What makes you think you were given the

money? I didn't specify the source. You could have earned it."

"I know it's a hypothetical situation, but you can't blame me for assuming I'd won the lottery."

*Only one ingredient so far,* Toshiro thought. And so it continued. The man's questions were vast and broad like mountains; the woman would struggle to climb them. The man relished watching her try, but when his fiancée did finally sit with an answer grasped in her palm, she was witty and resolute, and he loved it even more. Spring onions became children, tender chunks of pork became stories of humiliation, and with every question answered, the man would look at Toshiro as if to check he were still there. Toshiro could think of nowhere else he'd rather be. He was captivated, an insect drawn to the dazzling light that hangs in the distance. A feeling of warmth had begun to cruise through him, a warmth that had not been triggered by the heat of the night. Even so, sweat dripped from his brow; he kept a towel nearby and used it to wipe his face every minute or so, feeling rapt and light-headed. The couple were delighted with the noodle soup. They were relentless with their compliments; Toshiro wondered if they were trying a bit too hard to please him, but discarded this thought promptly. Wishful thinking. He started to piece together his anecdote for Harue – for when he got home later – and the words came easily. *They were elegant and romantic and fearless, this couple. They gorged themselves silly – wringing each other out and scooping themselves all up.*

"Let me get this straight," the man was saying. "You had to go to hospital? It was that far up?"

The woman was giggling uncontrollably.

"Yes! I feel guilty about it now – I wasted so much time that could have been spent saving lives. The nurses must have been ripping me apart after I left. I mean, who in their right mind shoves a bean up their nose?"

"Well, you were seven and probably showing off."

Toshiro didn't try to hide his laughter this time – he chuckled outright with the two of them, their faces shiny in the artificial light of the streetlamps. Why did Toshiro feel as if he had been drinking one too many glasses of *sake?* Laughter was infectious, he supposed, and he was dizzy with it, but not just the good humour; something about the pair was intoxicating. He wanted to go back home with them. Not in a sinister way, of course. He wanted to bring them back to his house, cook more ramen for them if they wanted it, and just exist together with them for a time. Just for a time. He felt the evening coming to an end, knew that they'd be making an exit sooner or later – the bowls were nearly empty now – and Toshiro realised he hadn't seen another customer all night, which was odd. Had he let them stick around for too long? Had their presence acted as a preclusion to the arrival of other customers? Toshiro wiped his face again.

"It's our last round," the man said, lighting a cigarette. Toshiro, surprised, watched the smoke curl up towards the night sky, was reminded of things wafting away. He suddenly felt anxious, the intensity of his desire for them to stay reaching new, unexpected levels.

"Can I get you anything else?" Toshiro asked, his voice clumsy between theirs.

"That's all, but thank you," said the man, glancing at his watch. "I suppose we'd better go, actually." He took out his wallet and began sifting through its contents.

Toshiro's heart skipped a beat. Had he not interrupted, the couple might have stayed longer. Feeling slightly faint, he wiped his brow for the umpteenth time.

"Of course, of course," he muttered.

But he wanted to witness the last round. He wanted so desperately to hear one last secret unleash itself into the night, to be the only person watching it detonate and then fizzle out just as quickly, to get another helping, another portion of this feast he had been unwittingly invited to. Now the spell was broken, and the couple were moving their limbs in such a way that suggested he'd never see them again, and he felt a burning sensation where his eyes were, remembered where he was and the fact that it was late and that he'd need to pack up the stall and drag it home in the insufferable heat. He barely acknowledged them as they left. He walked several paces and sat down where the man had sat, his whole body aching.

It was some time before Toshiro noticed Beppu. He wasn't sure if the man had been sitting there the whole time, but Beppu was gazing in the direction of the departed couple, his sharp jawline throwing a distinctive shadow across his neck. He then turned and looked at Toshiro, who gave the faintest of nods, willing the homeless man to come forward. Beppu normally kept out of everybody's way, but ever since Toshiro had offered him a hearty bowl of soup on a stormy evening several months ago, Beppu had turned up every so often, hopeful. He was no bother, did not really speak much, and Toshiro was glad for the company.

Now he was shuffling towards the *yatai*. Toshiro, in contrast, was not moving. He couldn't bring himself to.

"Did you see them?" Toshiro asked, though it was more of a statement than a question.

"I might be leaving Tokyo," Beppu said.

Toshiro thought about this. If Beppu left, it would be like he had never existed at Suidobashi. Toshiro didn't even know his first name, but he hadn't wanted to ask. He then realised he had never found out the names of the two lovers.

"I've been here for too long," Beppu explained.

"Like those customers," Toshiro murmured. Then: "Did they really stay so long?"

"I lost count of the number of trains passing."

A pause.

"Do you think you will ever leave?" Beppu said.

Toshiro stared into the distance.

"She was a painter. And I will never see a work of art again."

When Toshiro got home that night, he did what he normally did. He turned on the fans, drank several glasses of water, took a cold shower, and told Harue about his day. This ritual sometimes took him an hour (he was hobbling about now) but tonight was different. He went to the kitchen and took out everything from the cupboards, all the remaining ingredients left in the house, the pots, pans and utensils. He was tired, so tired, but he wanted to cook. He wanted to gather all the ingredients and pore over them as the man had done with his lover, as the woman had done with the man. He put all the things that Harue loved in the ramen, and talked about his thoughts and feelings as he did so. He talked about how much he loved Harue's paintings, about how he would always be bitter that the two of them had never had children (it was not his wife's fault, however – biologically they had been dealt a bad hand) and that he had once considered finding another woman who could. He cried as he said these things. He had once stolen money from his father when he had been angry at his father, and his father had blamed someone else. He had once had a dream of becoming a writer. This dream had been thwarted by the pull of a steady income and a lack of confidence. Toshiro talked about this and was relieved at how good it felt to do so. When the ramen was ready, Toshiro devoured his portion. He had not realised how hungry he had been. Looking over to Harue's bowl, he was not sad when he saw that her bowl remained untouched.

When he went to bed, he felt the familiar numbing sensation after gazing at the empty space beside his pillow. He wondered if that feeling would ever subside, even with a full stomach. Then he rolled over and dreamt of the lovers and their chopsticks, spring onions and smiles, a gallery full of vivid and fluorescent lashings of paint, steam rising, the trains rumbling past, a man leaving Tokyo.

# ABOUT THE AUTHOR

R. C. Hutchings is an author and teacher from London. She has been published as a young writer and currently has an Instagram page dedicated to all things writing and poetry. Follow her at @_rhiwrites.

Printed in Great Britain
by Amazon